THE HEART CHASER

BOSTON HAWKS HOCKEY
BOOK 6

GINA AZZI

THREE CITIES PUBLISHING LLC

PROLOGUE

LUCA

Six Months Earlier

A bead of sweat rolls over the swell of Abbi's breast, sinking lower and disappearing into the material of her dress. I can't tear my eyes away if I want to. Who am I kidding? I sure as fuck don't want to.

I bite my bottom lip and continue to stare, unashamed when she turns in my arms and grasps my chin, realigning my focus to her face.

"You're staring again," she murmurs.

"It's hard not to."

She tries to fight her smile but loses. "Well, stop being so obvious about it," she warns playfully.

I smirk and shift on the barstool, which is tough to do considering her ass is grinding against my lap as she reaches across the bar and picks up two more tequila shots that Pete, the bartender, placed down. Damn, I'm ready to get out of Taps and take Abbi Walsh back to my place, my bed, for round two. Night two.

A body bumps into my side and I turn, a lazy grin rolling

over my lips when I spot my captain's girl, Chloe. She's also Abbi's best friend and I can tell by the nervous way she tucks a strand of hair behind her ear that she's worried about her girl.

Ah, to have a reputation that precedes me. Usually I prefer it that way but tonight…tonight, I'm breaking my own damn rules. I never go back for seconds but something about this woman makes me want another taste.

Not just want…*crave*.

"We're going to head out," Chloe says, gesturing toward Austin. "Do you guys want to come with?" She keeps her eyes trained on Abbi and I press my lips together not to laugh.

"I'm good, Chlo. Swear it," Abbi replies. Good girl. I slide my hand higher on her leg, my fingers gripping at her inner thigh a smidge tighter than necessary. Her ass settles more firmly against my hard length and I cough back a groan.

"Don't worry," I tell Chloe. "I'll take care of our girl." I'll take care of her all right. Images of last night, taking Abbi in the center of my bed, up against the door to my closet, then again, in the shower, flicker through my mind.

Chloe leaves with Austin and a moment later, Abbi turns again, her lips just grazing mine. "You ready to get out of here?"

"Fuck yes."

She giggles, the sound sweet. But I'm not interested in sweet. I'm interested in tonight, this moment, with this woman. I signal for Pete to close out my tab and slip my phone from my back pocket to order an Uber.

Abbi and I step out into the sticky heat of July together. While I normally prefer the winters—I live in Boston, bred in Philly—right now, I'm grateful for the heat. Because Abbi Walsh rocks curves for days and they're barely concealed in the tight, crochet dress she's wearing like a second skin. It should look hideous, like something my Nonna Angie would knit. Instead, it's sexy as fuck, clinging to her curves. It's nude colored and by the hard nubs of her nipples, it's clear that she's got nothing on underneath.

I help her into the Uber and slide in beside her, my hand once again planting on her thigh. This girl is like a drug, one hit and I already want more. It's disconcerting, this feeling. I don't know whether to run from it or lean into it. But it's just one more night, right? Abbi's only in town for a bachelorette party weekend. Then, she heads back to Hoboken, New Jersey and I get on with my life: my family, hockey, and girls with no drama.

She checks her phone, oblivious to the thoughts running through my mind, which is a bit of an ego check. Usually, women are desperate for my attention. Hell, they even do stupid shit like make out with each other, to get it. But not Abbi.

Nope, this chick played it cool from the moment I met her, uttering some bullshit about being into players and not the game. A flicker of annoyance runs through me when I recall she doesn't watch hockey. How the hell does one not like the greatest game ever invented?

I narrow my eyes, studying her expression. Her plush lips have tightened, her carefree expression from Taps now pinched. I glance at her screen but the letters swim.

"More bachelorette drama?" I joke, since the party ended last night with all the girls going in different directions.

She sighs heavily and stuffs her phone back into the tiny bag she's toting around. "It's nothing. Just my boss. Work stuff."

I snort. "Work? It's"—I lean forward to glance at the time on the car's dashboard—"one a.m. on a Saturday night. Tell your boss to fuck off."

I expect her laughter but when she glances at her lap, I

know that whatever is going on is more than that. Curiosity flares through me but the uncertainty in Abbi's expression has me biting back my words. I get it; I'm not usually a sharer either. Who wants to discuss feelings and crap when we could spend our time doing better, more interesting things?

"Hey." I reach out, lifting her chin. "Forget work. Let's just have fun, okay?"

She holds my eyes for a long moment. So long I begin to feel hot under her scrutiny. And not hot and bothered hot. Hot like itchy hot…like Abbi can see past the veneer of bullshit I like to coat myself in so I don't have to do the whole feelings and crap bit.

"Okay," she murmurs finally.

I flash her a grin followed by a wink. It's a relief when she settles more firmly into my side and I wrap my arm around her shoulders, hold her close. Not that this will go anywhere but for tonight, it feels nice to have a woman like Abbi under my arm.

It feels a hell of a lot more natural than it's supposed to.

FUCK. My body is weightless. Right now, I'm not in my bed, my legs tangled in my duvet, but in the middle of the Atlantic, floating along the tops of waves. I glance out the corner of my eye at Abbi. Who is this sexy temptress who managed to make my body break apart like *that*?

How was I supposed to hold on when she shattered on my cock, calling out my name like I was some kind of god, her eyes wild and reckless? A small ring of vulnerability edged her irises, which should have scared the shit out of me. Instead, I reveled in it and let her trust push me over the edge.

I swallow thickly, reaching out to pull her naked body against my chest. I'm not usually a cuddler but Abbi's leaving tomorrow, and for the first time in my life, I want the night to extend well into the following morning. I want to soak up all these little moments I usually rebuff.

On my nightstand, her phone buzzes and she blows out a sigh.

A wave of jealousy rises in my gut, intense and unprecedented. I bite down hard, trying to dispel the unpleasant emotion. At least Abbi didn't answer the call.

I press a kiss to the back of her neck, my tongue darting out and catching her earlobe. She sighs, contentedly this time, and I savor the swell of pride that rises in my chest.

Buzz. Buzz.

"Who keeps blowing up your number?" I ask.

"Damn." She moves to answer it which irks me.

I flop back onto my pillow and watch as she swings her legs to the side of the bed and swipes the phone up, her movements jerky.

"I told you not to call me again," she bites out through clenched teeth.

At that, I sit straight up, moving toward her. But she tosses out a hand, keeping me at arm's length, which I both respect and despise. Is some dick giving her a hard time? Harassing her? Or is it a one-night lay who won't take a hint?

Unease followed by frustration blows through me and I'm instantly awake, all my former orgasmic bliss dissipating. Now, I'm on edge, tense and tuned into every little emotion that flits across Abbi's face.

Her dark hair hangs like a sheet down her naked back. All long, shiny locks I want to run my fingers through. I reach out and play with the ends of her hair, wanting to touch her in some way. Have her connected to *me* because I can't stand the thought of her having a one-night anything with someone else.

"I'm not joking around, Phil."

Phil? Who the hell is Phil?

"You're making things harder for me," she admits, her voice strangled.

In the next moment, she pushes off the bed and strides into the bathroom, the door closing behind her.

The vibe in my bedroom changes drastically, the temperature dropping as if all the heat went with her. I fall back against my pillow, my frustration spiking. More than anything, I want to stride into the bathroom and demand... what? That Abbi answer my questions? That we keep in touch after this weekend?

The door to the bathroom opens and I look up as Abbi walks toward me, full hips, pert breasts, and a scowl. My dick hardens beneath the sheet as a flood of desire hits me, my need to remind her just how good it can be between us skyrocketing.

"You okay?" I ask, genuinely curious.

Abbi tips her chin at me and climbs back onto the bed, swinging a leg over my body.

She collects my hands in hers and pushes them over my head, her hair and breasts swinging into my line of vision as she leans forward. "Ready for round two, Luca?"

I nod, my throat too dry to form words. I want to ask her what happened, but I can barely think when she rolls her hips over mine. Abbi Walsh knocked me off my game real fast and right now, I don't care. I want to fall in line while she calls the shots.

"Everyone calls me Panda," I admit for no reason.

The corners of her mouth curl. Not quite a smile but no longer a scowl. "I like Luca."

"I like it when you say it, too."

She lowers her face slowly and when her lips meet mine, I bite lightly on her lower lip, egging her on. She kisses me hard, passionately, and I revel in it, letting her set the pace this time. It's aggressive and delicious. Intense and fierce.

Shit. Being with Abbi Walsh leaves me reeling.

"You're ruining me," I pant out, half joking but half not, after we've both climaxed for the third time tonight.

She chuckles. "That's the point."

"Who's Phil?" I ask, my voice light, but I'm more than just curious. I'm fucking desperate to know who the hell he is and more importantly, what he means to Abbi.

She gazes at me over her shoulder, turning fully until her upper body is splayed across my chest. Her eyes catch mine again, searching. At first glance, they're ordinary brown. But on closer inspection, they're not brown at all. Flecks of gold, sprinkles of green, the tiniest infusion of blue… She's got eyes like a marble. "Phil's a long story," she says finally.

"You in trouble?"

"I hope not."

I frown, hating her vague responses when two weeks ago, I would have high-fived her for them. But not now that I'm *leaning*. Now, I want more. "What's going on?" I ask quietly, my fingers lightly swiping up her back.

She freezes under my touch before relaxing again. "I made a mistake. At the time, I didn't think… I never expected things to turn out the way they are." She shoots me a half smirk but her eyes are too big. A glint of fear rings her irises. "You ever do something when you knew better?"

I nod slowly, mentally flipping through the mistakes I've made. There's a lot but the latest is thinking I have a chance with the beautiful brunette before me. I have no clue how to be the kind of guy a woman like Abbi would want. She's motivated, intelligent, and sincere. It's only been two nights and the things I feel for her have ballooned into something bigger than the weekend. "Yeah," I murmur, tilting my head to study her. My thumb traces her lip. "But the worst was not being there for my family the way I should have, the way I knew I should have, when I went off to college. I knew my siblings counted on me for a lot, they have since my mom passed when I was in high school. But I wanted my freedom and when I finally got it, I went all in. Kind of left them behind." Regret colors my words. Even though I've since made up for that wild period of my youth, tenfold, showing up for Pop, my stepmom, and my brothers and sisters constantly, that slip in judgement still pricks at me.

"Your mom passed?" Her eyes widen, her voice dropping.

I nod. What the hell am I doing? I rarely, if ever, talk about my mom. I clear my throat. "I was fourteen."

"That must have been hard," she says and I'm grateful she doesn't flip me some apology just because it's what you're supposed to do.

"It was." I press my lips together but a moment later, more words slip past. "At the time, when I was first recruited to play Division One, I thought my actions were justified. By then, Pop had already remarried." I tip my head toward Abbi. "He married my high school English lit teacher, which is a whole other story. But Ms. Green was kind of my person, my sounding board, after Mom passed and when she started dating Pop..."

"Things got weird?"

"Definitely strained," I agree, hating how angry I was with Pop during that time. "It wasn't until later that I realized it was mostly selfishness on my part."

"Or coping," she says, surprising me. Her eyes take on a faraway look. "My parents died too."

"Both of them?" I ask in disbelief, her story shining my past in a different light. One a hell of a lot less bleak than I usually consider it.

She nods. "My mom when I was twelve. She was incredible." A soft smile touches her lips before it falls, a hardness lining her face. "My dad, well, he hasn't been in the picture in a long time. He walked out on us when I was eight for his new family, the one he was building when he was still married to Mom." She turns away and I can tell she's trying to school the expression on her face. When she speaks again, her voice is direct, hard and cold, like a bullet. "I heard from his other family that he passed two years ago."

My throat tightens, a wave of empathy rising. I don't want Abbi to think I'm pitying her, especially since I know how much it sucks to be on the receiving end of pity, but my chest squeezes at how much she's lost. My hand stills in the center of her back. "That sucks, Abbi."

"Tell me about it."

"Must have been really fucking tough."

She shrugs. "My gran raised me."

I wrap my arms tighter around her, hating that she stiffens. "Is she, do you see her often?"

She blows out a breath, relaxing slightly. "As much as I can. She's in a nursing home now. Her health has declined over the past few years. She's the closest person in the world to me and it's weird knowing that when she…well, it'll just be me then."

Swallowing becomes difficult as the emotion clogging my throat grows at Abbi's words. I have a loud, rambunctious family and while we're usually too involved in each other's lives, I've never considered the alternative. I've never even thought about if I didn't have my siblings and their kids around. "Have you ever reached out to your dad? Your…half-siblings?"

Her face falls and her eyes swim with moisture. What the hell am I doing? This is supposed to be casual and now… now, I feel sick that my questions are causing her pain. I'm about to tell her to forget it when she responds.

"Once," she whispers, wicking away a tear with a knuckle. "Sorry."

"Don't be. What happened?"

She lets out a big exhale, her eyes studying mine intently.

"I tracked him down. Showed up at his home. It was my junior year of high school and I just got my license. He didn't even live far away, only three towns over from mine. All those years, I thought he was in California or Texas or someplace different. I made up all these stories about him in my head, excuses to explain why he never came around, made an appearance at my birthday parties, spent a holiday with me. And he was right…there."

I pull her closer and kiss the side of her head as anger builds in my veins.

"I parked across the street and just…watched. His new wife was pretty. His kids were small. And after they had this picture-perfect dinner at their dining table, he came outside to throw out the garbage. I approached him and…I don't know why I'm telling you this. It doesn't matter."

"Yes, it does," I say, my tone soft. "It matters, Abbi."

She wets her lips. "He asked me what I was doing there. He asked if I have any respect for him, for his life, his family." She winces, and more tears fall. "He told me I was a mistake and my presence would mess up his life, the good thing he had going on. Basically, he discarded me as easily as the trash bag."

Fuck. My stomach clenches at the expression on her face. Hot anger burns through me and even though I never met her father, I hate the man who gave her life and didn't stick around to see her embrace it. "He never deserved you."

She bites her bottom lip, trying to force a smile. "You don't even know me."

"I know you deserved a hell of a lot better than what you got." What kind of man steps out on his family? On his kid? I frown as my sister Nikki's life flares to mind. My worthless brother-in-law left her a few months after their first child, Valentina, was born. My other sister, Justine, lost her husband too. But Dean was one of the greatest men I've ever known, and his being killed by a drunk driver cut my entire family off at the knees.

Abbi sighs and presses her palms against my chest. A wariness fills her eyes and I can relate; we're both sharing more than we bargained for tonight. "Sorry, I just made that a lot more real then—"

"No," I cut her off, tapping her ass. "You're just being honest."

She shrugs, her eyes serious. While I should change the subject, distract her from the too real thing we're doing right now, I move closer. I *want* her words. Her thoughts. Her goddamn feelings and crap.

"You ever want more than one night?" she asks, reading my mind. "More than just the moment?"

"We've spent two nights together," I remind her.

She bites lightly on my index finger and I pull my hand back, laughing. "Are we having *the* talk, Abs?"

At this, she laughs, amusement flaring in her eyes. "No, Luca. I'm not asking you how many women you've slept with."

"That's a relief." I grin saucily, but at the seriousness in her expression I continue to share. "But I thought *the* talk was more about commitment?"

Abbi chuckles, dipping her head in acknowledgement as something I can't read flares in her eyes. "Definitely not ready for that. You know me, I'm just over here keeping things light."

I laugh with her since we just had one crazy intense, serious conversation. "Yeah, that's you."

She smirks, but her eyes remain pinned to mine.

"To answer your question, not really. I know what my reputation is and I do nothing to help it. Women know exactly what they're getting when they climb into my bed." I wince at how the words sound when they're out in the space between us.

Abbi's eyes dim and my chest tightens, uncomfortable. I clear my throat and toss out more unexpected honesty. "But with the right woman, yeah, I'd want more. Doesn't everyone?"

Slowly, she nods. "I just don't want to be naive," she says quietly. "Every time I trust a man…" She trails off. "Well, it never works out the way I think it will."

I hate the sadness that streaks across her expression. I hate the failure that flares in her eyes because I've seen my sister Nikki wear it on too many occasions.

"Hey." I pinch her side. "You're not naive, Abbi."

"You barely know me, Luca."

I shake my head. "That's not true. I know that you growl when you—"

"All right," she cuts me off, her hand slapping over my mouth. But she's laughing and that makes me feel like I just saved a game by catching the puck at the buzzer.

I roll her until she's settled beneath me. Dipping forward, I drop a kiss to her mouth. "Everything you've showed me of yourself this weekend has been the opposite of naive. You're independent, you know what you want, and you're not afraid to ask for it. You're a good friend, putting up with that bachelorette bullshit. You're loyal, worrying about Chloe the way you do." I pause, realizing that I'm gazing into Abbi's eyes like I want to fall into them and stay awhile. I brush her hair back from her face. "Don't beat yourself up, babe. Not about things in the past that can't be changed."

I lower my head and kiss her again, wrapping her up in my embrace. I keep my arms around her as I doze off to sleep, the buzz of alcohol, the intensity of our connection, catching up with me.

I wake early the following morning, mostly from habit. I need to get up, get a run in, have a smoothie. But when I glance at my bedmate, with her tangled dark hair and long, black eyelashes, I don't want to leave the bed. *Her.*

It's an intense realization because it's the first time I've had it. I've seen firsthand how much love, real love, destroys a person. First, my Pop, when Mom died. Then, my sister, Nicole, when her husband took off. I've watched the loss of Layla devastate my teammate James and held my sister Justine as she wailed over Dean's lifeless body.

Of course, there's happy examples too—Noah, Easton, and Torsten come to mind. Jesus, even Cap is shacking up with Chloe now.

But when you're raised in a house overflowing with love and light, with laughter and fun, and the matriarch of the household, the glue that holds it all together, is suddenly gone, the shadow stamps out all the remaining glow.

I watched Pop fall apart until he met my stepmother. I watched Nicole break when she learned her husband was cheating on her while she was pregnant with their first child. Since then, I've stepped up for my family in all the ways that matter. I don't have the mental bandwidth to be a man for anyone else. Most days, I don't want to be. But today…

I brush Abbi's hair back from her forehead, grinning at the soft snore that whistles from her nose. I wish I didn't have so much fun with her this weekend. I wish I didn't like her so damn much. Because a part of me wants to see her again, even knowing it's a dangerous step. Could we keep in touch? Be…friendly? It's not like she won't be coming to Boston to visit Chloe.

When she's in town, could we kick it? Have some drinks and laughs together?

I chew the corner of my mouth, liking the way she looks in my bed. Liking her sexed-up hair and the makeup smudges underneath her eyes.

Her eyes flutter open and a slow smile covers her lips as she catches me watching her.

"You're checking me out pretty hard," she calls me out.

I smirk, crawling closer to her luscious lips. "I've got something else that's hard."

She squeals as I wrap her up in a giant hug and kiss her.

"I need to brush my teeth!" She pushes at my chest. "Morning breath."

I laugh and shake my head. "Not letting your ass out of this bed until you have to go."

She sobers for a second, stilling in my arms. "I had fun this weekend, Luca."

"Me too, Abbi Walsh. But it doesn't have to just be this weekend. You could, you know, reach out when you're in Boston."

"I could," she says slowly, lifting an eyebrow. Damn, I love how she even calls me out silently.

"I'll call you," I tell her, meaning it.

"We'll see," she says noncommittally.

"I mean it, Abbi. You're not walking out of here that easily," I half joke, wondering why the hell I'm complicating my life. Can't I just kiss her goodbye? No. I can't. Because I don't want her to leave.

"Are you for real right now?" she asks lightly, but her eyes search mine with a seriousness that causes the space between us to shift.

I shake my head. "You deserve a good man, Abbi. One who doesn't make you feel naive. One who keeps his word. Don't settle for less than that."

She draws in a sharp inhale, and I drop my head to kiss her lips.

I don't know why I say it like I could be that man. I'm not that guy and I know it the second the words are out of my mouth. But for her, I'd want to be.

The realization scares me because...Jesus, it's a lot. I don't do morning afters. I don't even do second-night stands. And everything that transpired between Abbi and me is a million times more than anything I've done in the past decade.

She leaves an hour later and for a bit, my condo feels empty without her presence. It's like she filled it up with energy, the kind Mom used to exude, and now that she's gone, the space plunged back into shades of gray.

I swear and force myself to go for a run. I need the workout and running helps clear my head. When I return, I strip my bed, suddenly desperate to wash the scent of Abbi—lilac and vanilla—off my sheets so it doesn't torture me.

My phone rings and I pick it up to talk to my sister. "Hey, Nikki."

"Luca?" Her voice is strangled and a cold fear drips down my spine.

"What's wrong?" I ask automatically.

"It's Pop."

"What happened?" I sink to the edge of my bed, the sheets pooling around my feet from where I tossed them to the floor.

"He had a heart attack."

I close my eyes, waiting for the words she hasn't said yet.

"The doctors think he's going to be okay but," Nikki sobs, "it's just so awful, Luca."

"Fuck." I swear, hanging my head. "How's Jenni?" I ask about our stepmother. Even before she married Pop, she was like a second mother to me.

"Not well."

"I'm getting on the next flight. Shit, Nik."

"I know. I know. Just, come home, okay? We need you."

"Of course," I say on autopilot. I'm already walking to my laptop, pulling up a search engine to find the first flight to Philly.

I leave the sheets on the floor, the condo a mess, as I throw together a bag and head to the airport. I spend the rest of the summer, until training camps start, in Philadelphia trying to get Pop on a new lifestyle routine. I take over his and Jenni's finances while he's out of work. I fill in as dad for my sisters' kids. I help my brother Robbie remodel his basement.

By the time I return full-time to Boston at the end of the summer, Abbi Walsh is a sweet memory. She's a reminder of a fun, exciting weekend I can never get back. She's a moment I savor on difficult nights. A woman who made me feel and want so much more than a weekend but ultimately, one who deserves more than I can give.

Abbi Walsh is a reminder that I don't do love. I only do heartbreak.

And I prove it because I never call her.

CHAPTER 1
ABBI

"Look who's banished to Boston now," I mutter under my breath, recalling my best friend Chloe's words when she moved to the city at the start of last summer. Now, she's happily in love with her boyfriend, Boston Hawks Captain, Austin Merrick. The man I need to thank for securing me this job as my life in New Jersey disintegrated.

I sigh, staring up at The Meadows, the ice hockey arena that houses the Boston Hawks Hockey franchise. It's going to be my place of employment as soon as I walk through those doors.

Snow skirts around me as the wind howls, blowing an icy blast straight through to my bones. But I don't feel the cold. My heart rate thrums in my temples, as nerves skate up my spine.

I just need to walk through those doors and find HR.

A car passes going well above the speed limit, sending a spray of melted snow over my heeled boots. They weren't the most sensible shoe choice, but they make me taller. More confident. Still, I don't budge.

Will I see him? On my first day in my new job, will my path cross with Luca Pandatelli's?

The thought causes bile to rise in my throat even though the likelihood is slim. But now that the thought has floated through my mind, a slew of others follow.

Did he tell his teammates that he fucked the new department head of Youth Outreach? That he worked her over so good, her body didn't just shatter, but some of her walls came down? That he left her with stars in her eyes when he kissed her goodbye and promised to call?

Except he never did. My chest aches at the reminder of Luca's rejection.

Will I walk into The Meadows and receive long side glances and under-the-breath quips like I did at my old job?

A blaze of anger rolls thorough me at *that* reminder. Getting involved with my boss, Phil Rickens, was a massive mistake for many reasons but the way he manipulated me out of a job is the one that hurts the most.

Phil's a retired NFL player. Every athlete I've ever dated, and there have been many, has lied through their teeth. But with the majority, I never expected more than casual fun. Only three managed to make me hope before showing their true colors.

First, my college boyfriend, the baseball player I was going to marry until he knocked up my sorority sister. Then, Phil when he said he was divorced but really meant separated and in marriage counseling. Now, they're expecting a child. Surprise! And lastly, Luca Pandatelli who kissed me goodbye with intention on his lips and a promise in his voice. *I'll call you.* Except he didn't.

I scratch my cheek and try to steel my shoulders. Gran's words—*dry your eyes, lift your head, and straighten your spine*—float through my mind but tears prick the corners of my eyes.

Losing Gran in early November was the final nail in the New Jersey coffin. With no job, no family, and no relationship to keep me in Hoboken, I leapt at the chance to start over in Boston with the Hawks franchise.

Being in Boston means being close to Chloe again but it also means dealing with Luca Pandatelli. I can't overlook that Luca built me up just as Phil started tearing me down. That for one weekend, he made me feel cherished and whole. That he didn't run from my oversharing or my tears but engaged in a real, meaningful conversation. His kindness, the empathy in his eyes, and the sincerity in his voice, made his subsequent dismissal downright painful. But I should have known better. Every time I trust a man, I get burned, and Luca is no different.

"You lost or somethin'?" a male voice with a Southern drawl asks and I turn, my breath freezing in my throat when I recognize Declan Yaeger, one of Luca's teammates.

I stare at him, my mouth opening and closing several times. Does he remember me from that weekend? From drinks at Taps? Does he *know*?

He frowns, squinting at me like he can't place my face. "Do I know you?" he asks after a moment.

I release an exhale. I can do this. I'm here for the job, for the fresh start it provides. I know Austin personally placed my resume in front of senior management and the Hawks owner, Scott Reland. I know I'm qualified for my new position, but I probably wouldn't have secured it so easily, or quickly, without the bit of nepotism that played in my favor. I swore I would start this opportunity the right way. Professional, polite, and focused on the work.

I smile and hold out my hand. "Hey, Declan, right?"

He nods, glancing at me uncertainly.

"I don't know if you remember me but we met over the summer at Taps."

"We did?" Panic ripples over his expression.

Damn, does he think we slept together? Is that all men think when they see me? Do I give off vibes of being an easy lay? An obvious target?

I nod, keeping my expression neutral. "Yes, I'm Chloe's

friend, Abbi. I accepted a job here in Youth Outreach. Today's my first day," I explain, glancing over my shoulder at the massive, imposing building.

Just walk through the damn doors already!

When I turn back to Yaeger, he's smiling broadly, relief in his eyes. "Abbi! Yes, of course I remember you. You and Chlo had a bachelorette party that weekend."

"That's right."

"Good to see you again," Yaeger says easily. "You want me to show you where HR is?"

My heart rate ticks up at the kindness in his tone. He doesn't know about Luca. If he does, he doesn't let on and for that I'm grateful. Some of my worry bleeds out and I nod again. "That would be great, if you don't mind. I don't want to hold you up."

"Not at all." He tips his curly head toward the front doors. "Come on. I'll introduce you to whoever we pass so you'll start off on the right foot."

I smile, my teeth flashing from my overwhelming relief. That's right. I'm starting off on the right foot. I fall into step beside Yaeger as we cross the street.

He tugs the door open and holds it for me as I slip inside, the warmth of indoors hitting me straight on. I unwind my scarf from around my neck and glance around the sterile hallway.

"Offices are this way." Yaeger points toward a stairwell.

I follow him up the stairs.

"When did you move to the city?" he asks.

"Friday," I say. "The past few weeks have been a whirlwind."

"Yeah, management is eager to kick off the Youth Outreach program with the start of the new year. The team is pretty pumped about it too. There's something special about connecting with kids, remembering how it felt to skate on the ice for the first time. Score a goal." He shoots me a crooked smile and I grin back as he holds the stairwell door open.

"I bet. I love working with kids. At my last job, I was in charge of the football programs so it's exciting to try out a new sport."

"Cool. Well, if you need any help with anything, don't be afraid to reach out. Any of the guys would be willing to jump in and support any new initiatives."

"Thanks," I say, meaning it. *This* is what I hoped for when I accepted this position. After things went south with Phil and me, no one wanted to work my events. It didn't matter that the downright hostile brush-off hurt the kids. My reputation was so damaged—home-wrecker—that not even a worthy cause could encourage my colleagues to do the right thing.

"I need a few days," a voice bellows from the open door to a conference room. But it's the sound of it that pulls me up short. Luca's voice hits me straight in the chest as memories of that weekend flood my mind. The pain in his tone, the rawness of it, scrapes at me and renders me immobile.

A deep sigh. "I know, Panda. I'm trying to work with you."

"You okay?" Yaeger asks, his hand finding the small of my back.

I shoot him a weak smile and shake my head. "Yeah, sorry."

"Coach—" Luca starts again.

A female cuts him off, "Panda, your new endorsement contr—"

"Fuck my contract," Luca's voice rings through the hallway as I fall back in step with Yaeger.

Yaeger shoots me an apologetic look. "We've all got a bit of an ego," he jokes.

I force a shaky chuckle just as Luca comes barreling out of the open door, nearly colliding with me.

"Shit," he swears, his arm wrapping around my lower

back to keep me upright as I teeter on my heeled boots from the impact.

Yaeger quickly steps behind me, his hand wrapping around my upper arm to steady me.

"Sorry," Luca breathes out. "I didn't see—" His eyes slam into mine and he freezes. The frustration in his deep, baby blues turns to ice. "Abbi?"

I shuffle back half a step, my body pressing more firmly into Yaeger's. He doesn't release his hold on my arm and in this moment, I'm grateful for that too. Seems like Declan Yaeger is going to be my first real Hawks friend, not counting Austin.

"Pandatelli," I say, relieved my voice doesn't shake the way my knees are.

Luca narrows his eyes, taking in his teammate's hand on my arm.

Yaeger gives me a little squeeze before dropping my arm. He points to a set of double doors. "HR is just through those doors, on the left. I need to take this." He slips his buzzing phone from his back pocket and shakes it at me apologetically. Before he answers, he asks, "You good?"

I hold my breath in my lungs for an extra beat before releasing it, reminding myself to breathe. "I'm good. Thanks, Declan."

"'Kay. See ya around, Abbi." Yaeger lopes off, raising his phone to his ear.

Luca continues to watch me, his gaze glacial. His jawline, deliciously shadowed in scruff, is hard enough to break glass. His lips are a firm line, as severely unrelenting as my new life outlook.

"What are you doing here?" Luca demands.

I roll my lips together. *Professional, polite, detached.* This is my new mantra when it comes to men I have history with. "I accepted a job," I say, professionally.

"Here?" he asks, incredulous.

I nod.

He narrows his eyes. "Why?"

I narrow my eyes back. Why? What kind of a question is that? "Because it's a good opportunity for my career."

Luca scoffs, pinching the inside corners of his eyes as if seeing me somehow ruined the equilibrium of his morning. I can't imagine how since he clearly never gave me a second thought. "Your career, huh?"

My uncertainty gives way to a current of anger that feels a lot safer than vulnerability. But I don't let it show, because, polite. "Correct. Now, if you'll excuse me." I move to sidestep him, keeping my spine straight and my chin held high.

But his arm darts out and he wraps his hand around my forearm, his eyes flashing with too many emotions to decipher. "Abbi, I..." he falters, frowning as he stares at me.

Detached. "See you around, Pandatelli."

I shake off his touch and push through the double doors.

CHAPTER 2
LUCA

I watch Abbi's hips swing as she walks away from me. She doesn't turn around. She doesn't even seem affected by running into me while I'm left here…playing catch up.

Why the hell is she here?

Guilt wracks through me about the way I left things the last time we were together. I kissed her goodbye and told her I'd call. And then my life went to shit and I preferred to keep the reminder of her untarnished. If I called, I only would have fucked things up the way I always do with women. Because I never want what they want. I never want the commitment and the monogamy and the future.

But with Abbi, I could have. No. I shake my head, as if to clear the preposterous thought. I told Abbi not to settle and that's exactly what she would be doing with me.

Besides, my family needed me and they trump everything.

But why is she working here? And why the hell didn't anyone tell me? Does Austin know? He must know. Chloe and Abbi are joined at the hip. There's no way she accepted this position without running it by him.

Hang on. Did he help her secure this position? Did he have a hand in this and purposely withheld the details from me? I frown, my anger redirecting toward my team captain which is pretty shitty since we're having an incredible season.

Fuck. My drama-free personal life, well, as it pertains to women at least, just got a hell of a lot more complicated. I stare at the closed double doors that lead to Human Resources. I never meant to lie to Abbi. It's just, after so many weeks holding my family together, too much time had passed. Too many things had changed to reach out to her.

Judging by her cool demeanor, I hurt her when she's the first woman I ever really gave a shit about hurting. And that sucks.

I blow out another sigh.

It's been one hell of a time lately and I was hoping that the new year would start off better. Considering Abbi Walsh just rolled back into my life, looking like she hates my guts, cozying up to fucking Yaeger, a dude I've been trying to wingman, blows that hopeful thought to smithereens.

I lean against the wall, pulling my phone out to check my messages. I scroll through them, a list of concerns from my siblings and their families. I glance back at the double doors.

Abbi would never be happy with a guy like me. Six months ago, maybe. But not since I stepped into the role I should have undertaken years ago. Not since I became Family Man Luca, which is fucking laughable because now, I'm even more emotionally unavailable than when I was just Playboy Panda.

But Abbi, with her hopeful eyes and her worry about being naive, played for a fool, deserves better than a guy who doesn't know the first thing about making a woman feel like a priority. Nah, the best thing I can do for Abbi is make her think that night meant nothing. That we were nothing more than a summer hookup, a bout in the sheets, a weekend of tequila shots and questionable decisions.

She deserves a man who will keep his word. And I'm clearly not that guy. Not when I'm already supporting more women than I can manage. My stepmother, my sisters, my nieces—are relying on me now more than ever.

There's no way in hell Abbi would want to come second to that. And she can't just be a casual fuck buddy. Not after that weekend. Not when we *shared* things.

Even though I lied to Abbi six months ago, it was for the best. I'd rather her hate me now, after one weekend, than despise me for not living up to the hockey player she built up in her mind.

Pushing off the wall, I enter the stairwell and bound down the steps. I enter the locker room and change quickly, desperate to get a workout in. Anything to quiet the thoughts in my mind. Something to pour my restless energy into. I pop in my EarPods, pick an intense playlist on Spotify, and work out until I can barely lift my arms.

Still, images of Abbi plague my mind.

"YO, you ever gonna tell me that Abbi Walsh is working here now?" I bite out at Cap when he enters the locker room.

Austin checks me with a hard look. "Didn't know I needed to run senior management's decisions past you, Panda."

I roll my eyes. "Come on, Cap. You could've given me a heads-up."

Austin leans against a locker and crosses his arms. "Or you could've called her and found out what she's up to all by yourself."

I snort out a laugh, narrowing my eyes at him. "You're kidding me, right? You're, what, not going to have my back now because you're fucking Abbi's best friend and—"

My words die a sudden death as Cap's arm cuts across my

windpipe. He shoves me hard against the lockers, his eyes angrier than I've ever seen them.

I hold up a hand and he eases the pressure against my throat, backing away.

"Fuck," Austin swears running a hand through his hair. He points at me. "Don't say shit about Chloe."

"I'm sorry," I say, because it was shitty of me to bring his girl into this. It's just, I'm hurt he wouldn't think to tell me about Abbi. Austin knows exactly what went down between us this summer. Is he angry with me about it? Is Chloe? Neither one of them let on and yet... "Why didn't you tell me?"

Austin sighs, lacing his fingers behind his head as he turns and stares at me. "Chloe and I swore we wouldn't get involved in whatever the hell transpired between you two. It's just, you've had a tough go of things. So has she. We thought it best just to be your friends and not...feed you info about each other or complicate things when it's clear you both want nothing to do with each other."

I frown. What tough go has Abbi had? And what does Austin mean it's clear we want nothing to do with each other? Did Abbi say that? Does she hate me for not calling?

Guilt burns through me, eating up my thoughts. Of course she hates me. I let her believe that our weekend would develop into more. I wanted her to expect something from me because when I kissed her goodbye, I intended on delivering.

"Whatever," I say, keeping my voice neutral. "A heads-up would've been nice."

Austin nods. "Well, she's head of Youth Outreach now."

My eyebrows lift. "Head? Of the program?"

"Yeah. She ran a lot of the football outreach programs for the New Jersey Kings for five years. She's more than qualified for the position. And Boston will be a good change for her."

I narrow my eyes. "Why?" I ask, even though the more important question is how the hell did I never ask what she does for a living? We spent two days wrapped up in each other and…she was right. I don't really know her at all. Shame flares in my chest and I lift a hand to rub at it.

Austin shoots me a look. "I'm not sharing Abbi's personal life with you. Just like I won't share yours with her. You want to know what's going on? Ask her."

I don't say anything and after a moment Austin sighs. "Look Panda, right now, the team's in a good place. We're having an incredible season. You really want to make a big deal out of this?"

"No." I don't. I just want to play hockey and be there for my family.

"Okay. So, we're good?"

"All good, Cap," I say.

"Other than a few outreach events, your path won't even cross with Abbi's. Unless you want it to?"

"I don't." I shut that idea down real fast. The best thing I can do for Abbi now is stay away. Just hold on to our weekend as a memory, a moment better left in the past.

CHAPTER 3
ABBI

PHIL

Don't get too comfortable in Boston, Abbi. You'll be back soon.

Bile rises in my throat as the image accompanying Phil's message comes through. It's me, slightly drunk, bending over his desk in a black lace thong. I'm glancing over my shoulder, giving him some serious smolder, my eyes begging for him to fuck me.

God, how fucking thirsty was I?

Disgust mixes with my anguish as I glare at the photo. Was I really that desperate for attention? For…love? A shiver wracks down my spine as the threat behind Phil's words registers in my mind. *Don't get too comfortable.* Is he planning on sharing these images? On blowing up the life I'm trying to rebuild in Boston after he decimated the one I created in New Jersey?

Helplessness that infuriates me rolls through my body. I drop my head back against the wall before sliding down to sit on the bench in the hallway of The Meadows. This is the last place I should be having any kind of emotional meltdown.

There are too many eyes to witness my panic, too many mouths to talk shit.

Tears burn behind my eyelids and I blink furiously. I drag in a breath and count to four before I release it. I'm fine. Everything is fine.

Straighten your spine. Lift your head.

A new pang cuts through my chest as Gran's voice floats through my mind. I press the heel of my hand against my breastbone until the sharpness dulls into an ache. God, I miss her. Building a new life without her in my corner is a lot harder than I thought. I close my eyes and draw in another slow inhale, trying to calm the nerves that buzz through my limbs.

I'm having a good week. Everything is fine. No one here knows about the photos. No one here even knows about Phil. Well, except for Luca but—

"What are you doing out here?" It's as if my thinking of him conjured his presence.

I look up, knowing he can read the tsunami of emotions bleeding through my expression.

Luca's blue eyes sharpen, concerned. "Hey, you okay?"

Fuck. The last thing I want is for Luca Pandatelli to pity me. In fact, I don't know if my cracked pride can handle it. I clear my throat and smooth out my expression. "I'm fine, Pandatelli." I stand and straighten my spine. Hardening my eyes, I lift my head and stare straight at him. "Everything is fine."

Luca frowns. His molars click together as he clenches his jaw. I know he doesn't believe me. "Look, Abbi, if you need to talk or—"

"I don't." The thought of him discovering my secret causes me to lash out. "And if I did, I wouldn't talk to you."

Luca jerks back in surprise before he widens his stance and crosses his arms over his chest. "Seriously? We're not even going to be civil?"

"I'm being incredibly civil," I say, keeping my tone even. I clasp my hands behind my back to hide the tremble of my fingers. "We work together. That's it."

"That's it?" he sneers, his concern giving way to anger.

I let out a slow exhale, relieved. Anger I understand; anger is something I can work with. "You're just another player," I remind him, my intent two-fold. He's both an athlete and a player of women and he knows it. "And I don't like games."

His eyes narrow into slits, confusion and frustration warring in their depths. I know he's recalling our first conversation and trying to understand the meaning behind my words. I scoop my purse up off the bench, refusing to help him.

Seeing Luca moments after reading Phil's message, looking at that image, has messed with my head. Right now, I feel too exposed, too vulnerable, especially in front of him. The last thing I want to do is give Luca more ammunition to mess with me, to interfere with my new position. Wasn't sleeping with him bad enough? Wasn't confiding in him about *things* even worse?

"What are you talking about?" he demands, shuffling toward me.

I take a step back and his eyes darken. No, darken isn't right. They smolder, angry and sexy and brimming with heat. He reaches for me, but I shake off his touch, both annoyed and intrigued by his passionate response.

Ugh. What is wrong with me? This, right here, is why I always end up in over my head. Because as much as my mind is screaming at me to back up, my body desperately wants to edge closer.

"Don't say shit you're not willing to back up," he growls.

I open my mouth, my head spinning for a good comeback when his phone rings.

He drops his gaze, giving me a momentary reprieve from

their intensity, and swears. He answers it immediately. "Jenni, I—"

I snort and shake my head, moving away from him. "Case in point," I spit out before turning on my heel and walking down the hall. I keep my head high as I pass into the stairwell. It isn't until I'm sitting in my car, warming my hands by the heat vents, that a sob rips from my mouth.

Luca Pandatelli could ruin me if I let him. Good thing I know better this time.

"HAPPY HOUR COMMENCES!" Chloe holds up her wine glass and I clink mine against it.

We're at Jolene's, a popular after-work watering hole, celebrating my first week of work.

I take a sip of the bold red, swirling the glass before placing it down on the high top. "How was your week?"

Chloe widens her eyes. "Seriously? How was your week? You're officially the Head of Youth Outreach for Boston Hawks Hockey! Come on, girl, tell me all about it. I'm sorry I wasn't here for you this week."

"Stop," I say, holding out a hand. Chloe's living her best life as an investigative journalist. She lucked out when her company transferred her to Boston but she frequently travels back to the head office in New York. "How'd your piece on Yemen go?"

"It's done." She flashes me a grin and sips her wine. "Janie was pleased with it."

"Good."

"Now that that's out of the way..." She grips my arm, her voice softening. "How was your week? How are you doing?"

I sigh, knowing my best friend is just looking out for me.

"It was good. I love the scope of the work and the team is fantastic. Everyone is really eager to launch more initiatives and the budget is generous. I'm excited to dive in."

"Excellent." She squeezes my arm before picking up her wine glass. "And your new place?"

"Perfect! It was really nice of Austin to help me find such an affordable apartment in a fantastic location."

"It wasn't a problem." Chloe flicks her wrist. "Torsten's retired now but he's more than happy to help out a Hawks employee when he can. Even though he's back in Norway, he and his wife, Rielle, still own a bunch of investment properties here in the city."

"Well, I love it. Being near the waterfront reminds me of Hoboken so it wasn't too big of a change."

"Good." Chloe beams. "You know, you're not too far from—"

I hold up my hand, cutting her off. I remember exactly where Luca's apartment is and I hate that it's within walking distance to mine.

Chloe sighs. A few moments pass in silence but I know my best friend. She's just angling for the best way to bring him up again. I'm about to tell her that I already saw him, twice, when she blurts out, "Luca."

I roll my eyes. "It's fine, Chlo. I ran into him—"

"Hey, Chlo." His warm voice rolls over my back, peppering it with goosebumps.

I freeze in my seat, dread and a flicker of excitement I ignore, swirling low in my stomach. What the hell? I've done a pretty good job avoiding Luca, knowing my self-preservation depends on it, for most of the week. While I can't avoid him forever, I needed some space to figure out my approach during my transition to Boston.

It hasn't changed. Professional, polite, detached.

"Abbi," he greets me.

I turn, keeping my face blank. Luca Pandatelli is standing

next to the high-top table looking like Brad Pitt in *Troy*. Delectable, sexy, and so damn fierce. I bite the corner of my mouth to keep from sighing. Strong shoulders pull the material of his sweater and a stubble I can recall scraping against my inner thighs taunts me. His eyes swirl like a summer storm, daring me to get lost in them.

I frown as I note the tiredness that clings to his face, deepening the lines in his forehead. His conversation with management from my first day flickers through my mind. Why does he need time off? Did something happen?

I don't care. I remind myself of this very important fact and clear my throat. "Hey, Pandatelli."

Across from me, I feel Chloe's eyes swing in my direction but I keep my gaze trained on Luca. In fact, I'm so focused on *not* studying how irritatingly good-looking he is to notice the petite blonde until she sidles up to his side. "I got us a table in the back," she chirps.

Now, my eyes redirect their study to her. She's beautiful in one of those effortless ways. Sun-kissed hair in the middle of February, wide blue eyes, a waist the same diameter as my thigh. She looks like an eager-eyed college kid. A wave of hurt clogs my throat but I swallow it down, letting this scenario remind me why I can't keep dating athletes. I just end up hurt and I'm tired of handing over my control like some flighty girl when I'm striving to be an independent woman.

I cling to being polite and detached. "Enjoy your drinks." I dismiss him, turning back to Chloe's bewildered expression.

"Uh, it's good to see you, Panda," she murmurs.

"Yeah," he says, his voice hard. He raps his knuckles against our table once but I ignore him until I see his back recede in my peripheral vision.

"What the hell, Abs?" Chloe asks.

I pick up my wine glass and take a long drink, wetting my dry throat. "What?"

Her eyebrows nearly touch her hairline. "You guys are… intense."

I snort. "No, we're not. Luca Pandatelli and I are nothing."

She sighs. "Look, I'm sorry things—"

I hold up my hand to cut her off and toss a declaration out into the universe. "I'm done with athletes, Chloe. If I was smarter, I'd probably swear off all men. But Luca and I now work for the same franchise and I've learned firsthand that you don't play where you work. Besides, Luca and I never had a chance in hell. What we had was a weekend. Two really great nights filled with smoking hot sex." I shrug. "From now on, I'm not mixing my work life and my personal life. I'm just…being professional."

Chloe lifts a skeptical eyebrow. "So, you're open to dating? Just not anyone who works for the Hawks?"

I shrug. "I'm always open to dating. Just…keeping it casual. Sex, no strings. Nights, no days."

She narrows her eyes at me. "And how is this any different than the shit you've been doing since after college?" Her forehead wrinkles. "You haven't dated a man for real since Kent."

Just hearing his name causes a ripple of unease to roll through me. Kent Ritters was my college boyfriend. He was the starting pitcher at Columbia University, an All-American type with a smile that could melt the coldest of hearts, and the man I thought I was going to marry. After my father, he's the first man to break my heart in what proved to be a series of failed relationships, by impregnating one of my sorority sisters our senior year.

I polish off my wine and shoot my friend a grateful look when she orders us another round.

"I can't keep doing this, Chlo."

"Doing what?"

"Dating athletes, or screwing them, whatever, and thinking something real is going to come from it."

"I agree."

"You do?"

She nods, tugging on the end of her hair thoughtfully. "You don't date them, Abbi. You don't really date at all. But"—her eyes glitter—"what if you did? What if you went on, real, actual dates, with men who are out of the sports world? Just regular guys with regular jobs for a regular dinner."

I wrinkle my nose. "Sounds boring."

"No"—she shakes her head—"it sounds safe. And you're not attracted to safe."

I snort.

"But, after the year you had, safe might just be what you need."

I thank the server for my second glass of wine and take a sip. Glancing around the room, my eyes snag on Luca. He's sitting in the back corner, grinning, as the blonde beside him laughs softly.

Ugh. He's so arrogant, sitting there like everyone should bow at his feet. I bet the blonde does.

He looks up and his eyes latch onto mine. His jawline tightens. I narrow my gaze but he doesn't look away, if anything, his stare hardens and his eyes blaze.

Luca's look alone causes my body to tingle. Images of that weekend flare to life in my mind. The way his hands felt on my skin, the way he made me laugh even as my world started to crumble.

Luca Pandatelli rolled into my life like a hurricane. He knocked me off-balance, drenched me with hopeful ideas, and left me devastated when he was done. His rejection, not a surprise given my track record with men, hurt more than it should have. That's the part that bothers me most. That I *trusted* him, almost implicitly, when I don't trust. I wanted to give him a real chance when I usually make a man work for it.

I turn away from him. "Maybe you're right," I say.

"Of course, I'm right." Chloe rolls her eyes. "Leave it to me."

"You don't have to—"

"Trust me, I do. You're my best friend and you're in a new city. My city. The least I can do is introduce you to new people. If you don't want to think of it as dating, then don't. It's just you, a hot, single, independent woman, meeting other hot, single, boring men in a new place for a meal."

I laugh and nod. "All right. One date."

"Three."

"This isn't a negotiation, Chlo."

"You're right. This is a new outlook. Three dates. Just dinner."

In the corner of my eye, I see the blonde tap a glass against Luca's in a cheers. I look away before I have to witness them do anything gross, like kiss. Anger beads in my bloodstream and my eyes burn, which is stupid because I don't care what Luca does. I'd be fooling myself if I thought him to be a saint these past six months. Just because no man in a twenty-mile radius wanted to come near me didn't mean *he* was going without. Just because Gran's death ripped me wide open and I gave off emotional train-wreck vibes to everyone I talked to —both men and women—doesn't mean Luca's been sitting at home crying into bowls of chocolate chip mint ice cream.

"Okay," I say to Chloe, meaning it this time. "But let's just start with one and take it from there."

I'm no longer in New Jersey. Fortunately, my shameful reputation hasn't followed me here. Besides, maybe Chloe's right. Maybe a boring, regular guy with a safe and steady job is just what I need.

Lord knows the alternative hasn't caused anything but heartache for far too long.

CHAPTER 4
LUCA

"Y‌ou sure you don't need me this weekend?" I ask my sister Justine over the phone.

"No, really. I'm okay," she says.

I sigh, pinching the bridge of my nose. While part of me is relieved, another part of me is worried. Flying to Philly every chance I can is taking a toll on me. Physically, it's a lot, and emotionally, it's draining, but if Justine needs me on the one-year memorial of Dean's death, I'll be there, my contract be damned.

"You were just here last weekend," she reminds me. "You paid your respects to Dean then."

"I know but…"

"You can't keep doing this, Luca. Flying back and forth, showing up at the boys' hockey games, bringing Laura flowers after her dance recital… It's sweet and I really appreciate it. But it's too much. You have a career, your own life. You can't keep putting it on hold for us. We're all managing just fine."

Her words are a salve to the guilt I've been buried under since Pop's heart attack. After Dean died, Pop stepped in big time to be a father figure, a role model, to Justine's three children. But since Pop's surgery, I've tried to fill those shoes. And damn, they are some pretty big shoes to fill, especially since Dean and Pop were two of my role models. "How's Pop?" I ask instead.

"He's getting stronger. Jenni says he's doing really well on his new diet and he's sticking to the PT. We're okay, Luca. I promise."

"If you need me, for anything—"

"I'll call," she promises. "You're going to make some woman very happy one day."

I snort. "I doubt that." I think about Abbi and the hardness in her eyes, the splotchy red circles on her cheeks, when she saw me at Jolene's with Carmen. For a moment, I read the jealousy in her expression, and it provided me with a strange sense of relief. In fact, that flicker of envy is the only thing that kept me from introducing Abbi to Carmen, my college teammate's little sister, who has become like another kid sister to me since she started attending Boston College three years ago. I take her out for a bite at the start and end of every semester and check in with her from time to time since her family is far away in Utah.

Seeing Abbi at Jolene's messed with me. All of a sudden, she's everywhere I turn, a sickening reminder of just how badly I messed up last summer. I don't know what's worse. The fact that Abbi's distant toward me, acting like we didn't share a sexy weekend together, like we didn't exchange some serious conversation, or that when she does look at me, there're too many conflicting emotions she's trying to lock down just under the surface.

I tune back in to whatever my sister is saying. "For dinner."

"Huh?" I ask.

She sighs. "Robbie's up for a promotion."

"Right," I say, remembering that my brother was angling for a promotion at the Philadelphia police department where he's an officer.

"If he gets it, you can come for that dinner. It will be a happy occasion, a celebration, instead of all the depressing things our family's been dealing with."

"True."

"And, I was saying, you should bring a woman."

"A woman?" I snort.

"Don't pretend to be a saint. I see the internet gossip."

"You shouldn't read that shit. And these women are only for a one-night thing if you get what I'm saying."

My sister swears at me. "Mama and Jenni raised you better than that."

Her words cause my stomach to ache. She's right; they did. But, they also didn't have to step up for everyone else all the time to know how impossible it is for me to have a real relationship. "I'll be there. No woman." I shut it down.

"One of these days, Luca…"

"On that note, I'll let you go."

My sister laughs. "Call Nikki. Valentina has bronchitis and—"

"I ordered her new inhaler."

"That was nice of you. We don't say it enough, big brother, but we couldn't do it all without you."

"It's nothing," I say, the thread of shame in her voice tugging at my heart.

I'm one of five kids and, other than my brother Ricky who is serving in the Army and stationed in Texas, I'm the only one to leave Philadelphia and financially level up. There's not a damn thing I wouldn't do for my family and I hate when they make it seem like they couldn't live without me. Because they're all smart, resilient, hardworking people. It's just that I can guard a hockey goal better and that's not exactly the noble, awe-inspiring job they make it out to be.

"Talk to you later, Jus," I say.

"Love you, Luca."

"Me too." I end the call and move to toss it onto the kitchen island.

Before I do, my attention snags on a new message.

NOAH

> Hey, New BHH outreach is having its first event in two weeks. Signed you up.

Of course he did. As much as I want to be involved in the team's new initiative to bolster hockey participation among Boston's youth, will my presence ruin Abbi's kick-off? Will she even want me there?

NOAH

> Also, pizza and video games at my place tonight? Indy's got a girls' dinner. I've got Emmaline. Come through.

LUCA

> Okay. See you in a bit.

A swell of gratitude toward Noah stamps out some of my previous annoyance. He's a good dude, super inclusive, and has reached out several times since Pop's heart attack. Since I've been spending so much time in Philly, I've barely kicked it with the guys unless it's right after an away game and we grab a bite.

Besides, now that Noah's a dad, he's been trying to watch the baby more when we're not traveling so Indy can have a social life. What that means is he usually employs the rest of us in babysitting duties with promises of pizza, wings, and beer. Clearly, it works.

And, Justine's right. I do need to keep living my life. It doesn't mean I'm not putting my family first. I'll still drop everything to show up for them and they know it.

I take a quick shower and tug on some ripped jeans and a sweater. Swiping my winter coat, I head over to Noah's.

I knock on the door to his and Indy's ridiculously cramped tenement apartment and shuffle back a full step when Abbi Walsh greets me.

When she sees me, her smile dims. "Hey."

"Hi," I say, placing my hand in the center of the door so she can't slam it in my face.

She narrows her eyes. "You coming in?" She moves to the side.

I sigh and study her, noting the smudges under her eyes. She's exhausted. What the hell happened the other day at The Meadows? Is she in trouble? "How've you been?" I ask slowly, wondering if she'll give me an inch.

Abbi rolls her eyes and I press my lips together, both annoyed and impressed that she won't even give a damn millimeter. "Fine. You?"

"Abbi, look—"

"It's fine," she cuts me off, having no idea what I was even going to say. And it's obviously not fine since the look in her eyes could rival a dragon's.

"Noah signed me up for your first event," I blurt out.

She nods. "I saw. You coming?"

"You want me to?" The last thing I want to do is make her nervous or uncertain about her first event. I'm not trying to throw her off her game.

Her expression softens slightly. "Of course. I want what's best for the kids, for the program."

"Then I'll be there." It seems like a truce of sorts but in the next instant, she turns away and I'm not so sure.

I follow her into the apartment, slapping greetings with the guys and saying what's up to Indy and Chloe.

"I just ordered pizza and wings," Noah informs me, tossing me a beer.

"Where's East?" I ask, referencing Noah's brother and one of our wingers.

"He's in a meeting. He'll swing by afterwards," Austin explains. "Yaeger and Sims are coming through too."

I nod. I've been really proud of Easton Scotch for turning his life around. After his second stint in rehab, and finding something special with Claire Merrick, he's got a good thing going.

"Claire?" I ask, looking around. No way the girls are going out to dinner without the life of the party.

"We're going to pick her up." Indy flicks a wrist. "She still refuses to buy a car but I think it's just so she never has to be DD."

I grin and Abbi laughs, the sound causing me to look at her again.

Her eyes are that same marble swirl but she looks happy and even though it shouldn't matter, it makes me happy to see her here, among friends, smiling.

"I got it!" Indy snaps her fingers and points at Abbi.

"Got what?" Chloe asks, placing her phone in her purse.

"Aiden," Indy states.

Austin swears under his breath.

"He's perfect," Indy continues, oblivious to Chloe's wide eyes and Austin's sharp look. "I don't know why I didn't think of it sooner."

"Think of what?" Noah asks, turning to glance at his girl.

"A man for Abbi!" she announces, excitement and exasperation in her tone.

Austin's neck snaps in my direction and then Abbi's.

My body locks down and a sick feeling explodes in my stomach. Fuck. Abbi's thinking of dating? I mean, of course she is. Why the hell shouldn't she?

But when we hooked up, there was that mess with... what's his name? Phil. Yep, that's it. Guess she kicked him to the curb. The realization makes me happy for about point two seconds before Indy's words sink in. Abbi Walsh is single and ready to get back out there.

I turn to look at her but she avoids my gaze. "Who's Aiden?" I ask.

"My best friend," Indy says. A cry sounds through the baby monitor and she makes a face. "That's our cue, ladies. I'll tell you about him over dinner." She passes Abbi her coat.

Abbi shrugs into it and I try not to stare. But it's hard because she looks hot. Real hot. Skintight leather leggings, a cropped maroon sweater, and sexy-ass boots that fold over her knee. Her coat is camel colored and cashmere. She pulls her long hair out of the back of her coat and I nearly groan as the scent of her shampoo, sweet vanilla, floats my way.

Why the hell does she look so good for girls' night? Does she have plans afterwards? Plans with a guy?

Jealousy swirls in my stomach.

"Baby, can't you change her before you go?" Noah asks Indy, pointing at the screen of the baby monitor where Emmaline turns in her crib.

Indy laughs and kisses Noah on the cheek. "Don't wait up."

Noah groans as Austin, Chloe, and Abbi chuckle.

But I don't laugh because I feel like fucking screaming.

I'm sorry! Don't you see it's better this way? You deserve more than I can offer.

Instead, I ignore Abbi completely as she stalks past me toward the door. Her scent wafts over me, the heat of her body ripples over mine, and then she's gone.

Austin cuts me a sharp look but doesn't say anything. When Noah reenters the room with baby Emmaline, I'm grateful as hell that no one besides Chloe and Austin know what transpired between Abbi and me over the summer.

The last thing I need is the team getting on my case for treating Abbi like shit. Because it's clear that they already like her. The way she answered Noah and Indy's door like they've been friends for ages, the way Yaeger stepped up for her in the hallway last week, are little signs that if my teammates knew the truth, they'd think I'm an asshole.

I've never tangled up with a Hawks employee before. And definitely not with a girl in the group's inner circle. Right now, Abbi Walsh is both. If I needed more reasons to stay away, I just found them.

CHAPTER 5
ABBI

y first event in my new role occurs two weeks after Chloe brings me into her circle of friends. Dinner with Indy, Claire, and Chloe is a turning point, a reminder that I'm now living life on my own terms.

Even Luca's presence can't overshadow the fun I have. By the end of the night, I eagerly agree to a date with Indy's friend Aiden. My first date happens to land on the same day of my first professional event, which needs to be moved up at the last moment due to an impending snowstorm.

I shake out my coat and scarf once I'm inside the high school gym, where the Hawks are donating hockey gear and jerseys to the JV and Varsity teams. As events ago, it's pretty straight forward, but since it's my first one with the Hawks, a zing of nerves works down my spine.

"Where do you want us?" Noah smiles at me broadly as he and Luca enter the gym from the opposite side.

The tables, pamphlets, and projector highlighting Hawks players, their top performances, and their backstories, is already set to go.

"Hey, guys!" I wave, keeping my eyes trained on Noah. "Thanks so much for coming. The bell rings in another fifteen minutes or so and then we should be swarmed with current players as well as other athletes who are on the fence about giving hockey a go."

"And the ones who just want to take a selfie," Luca quips.

"Right," I say. Modest, that one. I gesture toward a little table I set up with coffee and doughnuts for the coaching staff and people helping out to set everything up. "Help yourselves."

"Thanks, Abs." Noah moves toward the table. "Emmaline woke up three times last night. I need the extra caffeine."

"Have at it," I tell him. I restock a pile of pamphlets on a table, making sure they're perfectly neat.

Noah's phone rings and he moves toward the door to take the call, a coffee in hand.

The moment Noah clears the doorway, the atmosphere in the gym shifts. The air seems to tighten, heavy with tension, thick with awkwardness.

In my peripheral vision, I watch as Luca sits on a table, his feet still planted on the ground due to his height.

"Not even gonna say hi?" he asks.

"Hello," I grunt.

He snorts. "Wow. Didn't take you for spiteful."

His words hurt just as much as they anger me. "You didn't take me for much of anything," I mutter under my breath. Turning toward him, I place my hand on my hip and glare.

Luca's lips quirk upward but his eyes darken. "Just say what you mean, Abbi."

I shake my head. "Nothing, Pandatelli."

"What happened to Luca?" he asks mockingly.

"What happened to 'I'll call you'?" I shoot back, internally wincing at how much that makes me look like I care. But I don't. Care, I mean. Tonight, I have a date with a kind, respectable entertainment lawyer. I shouldn't take the bait and let Luca rile me up with bullshit from over six months ago.

He blows out a sigh and for a moment, a streak of regret blares over his face. His eyes soften, ringed in apology.

My hand slips off my hip and I hold my breath.

Is he going to apologize? Is he going to explain himself? Is he going to give me…something?

As quickly as it appeared, his regret is gone. His eyes shutter over and his expression hardens, like stone. "That's what this is about? Abbi, it was one weekend. And yeah, it was fun. The sex was hot. But come on, babe? That was months ago and you said it yourself, we work together now." The blasé veneer of his words, the dismissal in his tone, paired with my own logic, cuts. I hate that I still care; I hate that months later, his rejection still hurts.

I look back down at the pamphlets, my fingers playing with the edges of the papers. The back of my nose burns and I take a long moment to quiet the emotions flooding through me. I gain control of the tears that collect in the corners of my eyes.

I let the hurt from his brush-off morph into anger instead. Anger is safer. It's a hell of a lot more effective too. Slowly, I harden myself to Luca Pandatelli. When I glance back up, it's not even him sitting on the edge of the table, smirking at me.

It's Phil. And my college boyfriend. It's my father, the man who was supposed to love me unconditionally, but dropped me like a hot potato when a woman younger than my mother spread her legs for him.

"You're right," I say, my voice a hell of lot more even than I feel. For that, I'm thankful. "It didn't mean anything. We're here for an event," I remind Luca and myself, clutching at my professionalism with two hands. "Let's focus on that, on the kids. We'll just leave the past in the past. There's no need for us to mention it again. In fact, outside of professional functions, there's no need for us to talk at all."

Surprise flares in Luca's eyes as he realizes he miscalculated this exchange. His little performance, playing casual and flippant, backfired. I shake my head. As much as I hated it when he said it, Luca was also right. We work together now. He should only exist in my professional sphere. Besides, I've been burned too many times to go down this path again, to even entertain notions of tangling up with a professional athlete.

"Abbi," Luca's voice is low and this time, the apology is clear. Too little too late.

"Final bell just rang," Noah announces, clapping his hands together as he reenters the gym.

"Great," I say brightly, turning away from Luca. I walk toward Noah, explaining a few things and gesturing toward the end of the gym where the hockey gear is stored.

I feel Luca's eyes on my back, prodding me, but I don't give in again. Instead, I focus on the event. I engage with the students, the faculty, and coaching staff. I do my job with one-hundred percent of my focus.

As students trickle out and the day winds down, I grin at Noah's enthusiasm over it.

"That was awesome. I love talking to kids about hockey. They're gonna have a good team this year. Coach runs a tight program," he says, looking around the gym.

"Yeah. Today was fun," I agree. "Thank you so much for coming. Having you two here makes all the difference when it comes to getting kids, especially players, excited about the season and the future."

"Anytime, Abbi." Noah looks at me. "I mean it."

"Thanks, Noah." I move toward a few of the guys who are starting to repack extra equipment and break down tables. "I'm going to talk to them for a few."

"No worries, I need to take off anyway. You good?" Noah asks me.

"Absolutely. Have a good night. Say hi to Indy and kiss those sweet baby cheeks for me." I wave, walking away from Noah and Luca.

I have a few words with the guys and thank them for their help. When I turn back to collect my coat and purse, I'm surprised Luca is standing there, waiting for me.

"Abbi," he starts again.

"Have a good night, Pandatelli." I breeze past him, picking up my coat and slipping it on.

He sighs loudly but I don't turn around.

"You need a ride?" he asks after a moment.

I wind my scarf around my throat, pulling out my hair and fixing it to fall around my shoulders. I paste on a smile and spin around. "No, I don't." I start to walk toward the gym doors that lead out to the parking lot where Aiden is meeting me.

"I didn't see your car." Luca narrows his eyes.

"I got a ride." I pass him.

At the last moment, his hand darts out, giving me déjà vu of that day in The Meadows hallway. This time, he grips my upper arm.

I glance at his fingers around my arm before shooting him a dirty look. "Is there a problem?" I ask.

"Don't be like this."

"Like what? I thought you prefer drama-free?" I keep my voice light. Detached.

Luca growls. "We're going to be working together. We should at least be able to…talk."

"We're talking right now," I say through clenched teeth, once again dropping my gaze to his hold on me.

He drops his hand and I shake my arm, resuming my walk. "Have a good night, Pandatelli."

He swears behind me but I don't turn around. Because at that moment, the door to the gym opens and who I can only assume is Aiden Hardsin, Indy's best friend, steps into the gym.

As soon as he sees me, he smiles and damn, he's good-looking. Tall, with broad shoulders, and a trim waist. His blond hair is cut short on the sides and styled on top. Warm blue eyes meet mine and he smiles. "Abbi?"

"That's me." I grin back, extending a hand. "It's good to meet you, Aiden."

"You too. Indy was very clear when she told me you like steak and wine."

I laugh before nodding. "I do, but we can keep it casual. You don't have to go all out."

Aiden's eyes flare with amusement. "What if I want to? I hope you don't mind I made reservations at a steakhouse."

I grin. "That sounds good to me." I fall in step beside him.

Right before we reach the door, Luca clears his throat loudly and Aiden and I both stop and turn around.

"Hey, man." Aiden lifts a hand in greeting.

Luca flips his chin at Aiden in acknowledgment but his eyes are trained on me. Electric blue, they glare with an intensity that unnerves me.

Instead of reacting, I school my features, flip my chin back and step out into the cold February night with Aiden beside me.

CHAPTER 6
LUCA

I watch Abbi walk away with my heart in my throat. My hands curl into fists and a strange type of dread, similar to the flare of panic I felt when I learned about Pop's heart attack, settles in my stomach.

I didn't expect Aiden Hardsin to look like…well, a good-looking dude. Or to be so damn nice. I've heard about him for more than a year. As Indy's best friend and Claire's buddy to check out musical talent, Noah and Easton have referred to him on more than one occasion.

Every time, they have nothing but good things to say about the guy. That he's a stand-up dude, genuinely likable, and chill. That smile he gave Abbi wasn't chill or casual. No fucking way. He looked at my girl, at Abbi, like he couldn't wait to wine and dine her.

And then what? Will she go home with him tonight?

I hop off the table, a restlessness running through my veins. I pace the gym floor, watching night fall through the old windows. I should go home. It's supposed to start snowing soon.

Shit. If Abbi goes home with this guy, will she spend the whole weekend tangled up in his sheets, snowed in and happy about it? The thought unnerves me and I swear loudly, pulling out my phone.

The usual messages from my family members, voicing concerns and asking for advice, populate the home screen. I flip through them ensuring that nothing is urgent—nothing is—and dial Austin.

"Panda?" he answers.

"Where's Indy's friend taking her?" I demand.

"Jesus," he groans and I can hear the frustration in his tone. "What happened to moving on?"

"I'm curious."

"Aiden's a good guy."

"So I've heard," I say dryly.

"If you're not going to step up for her, you should be happy she's dating a decent man."

"Going on a date isn't the same as dating. Where's he taking her?"

Austin sighs. "Carter's."

I whistle. "So, he's for real?"

"He's for real," Austin confirms, turning my frustration into concern.

What if Abbi likes Aiden and they hit it off? What if they become a couple, a *we*, that I have to see at functions and games and team events?

The thought hits me like a slapshot. Fuck. I fucked this up. I thought Abbi would react to my bullshit tonight. Give me some anger, give me some emotions, give me something to work with. Instead, she shot me down cold and walked away with her head held high. Right into the arms of charming, decent, likable Aiden.

"Either man up and do something about it or let her go. She's deserves some peace after the shit she's been through," Austin says cryptically.

"What—" I start but he cuts me off.

"Sorry, Panda. You'll have to talk to Abbi." He clicks off and I stare at the phone in disbelief.

Cap just hung up on me? Is he serious? What the hell happened to bro code?

I pace the gym floor for a long moment, my thoughts wild, my emotions too jumbled to sort through. As my anger, toward Abbi, toward the situation, toward myself and my own shortcomings, heightens, I do something rash. Rash and stupid.

I pull out my phone and call Carmen.

"Hey, Panda," she answers on the second ring.

"Hey. You busy tonight? Want to grab dinner?"

Carmen laughs. "Uh-oh. What's wrong?"

I swear and grip the side of my neck, annoyed that my twenty-one-year-old pseudo sister can read me so easily. "Remember the girl from Jolene's?"

"The one you couldn't stop staring at?" Amusement laces Carmen's tone and I wince.

"She has a date tonight," I admit.

Carmen sucks in an inhale. "Luca Pandatelli, you cannot crash that girl's date."

"Why the hell not?"

Carmen groans. "You really like her, huh?"

"Obviously."

"If you get a chance with her…"

"I'm not going to fuck it up," I promise, hoping she'll put me out of my misery and just come eat a damn steak with me at Carter's.

"Fine. I'll go."

"Thank you," I breathe out, relieved. "I'll pick you up in ten."

I end the call and pull on my winter parka. On the walk to my car, I call Carter's for a last-minute reservation. Given the inclement weather advisory, I'm relieved they had a few cancellations and can squeeze me and Carmen in this evening.

I pull up to the curb in front of Carmen's apartment and am relieved she's already waiting outside.

She slides into the passenger seat and jabs a finger in my direction. "You owe me."

I roll my eyes. "I picked your drunk ass up on your twenty-first birthday and didn't tell your brother you puked in my car. I owe you shit." I ease my SUV in the direction of the popular steakhouse.

Carmen snorts. "Fair. Then, we're even. I don't like doing shit like this. That girl—"

"Abbi."

"Abbi looks really nice. And she kind of glared at you like you already messed things up with her."

"I did."

Carmen huffs and settles back in her seat. "You really think crashing her date is going to make her want to hear you out?" I hear the skepticism in her tone and bite back my smile.

"Absolutely not," I admit, chuckling. "But I don't care. I just need to see her."

"Damn, Panda." Carmen looks over, her eyes wide. "I'm definitely not telling my brother how whipped you are."

I flip her my middle finger. "Appreciate that, kid. And thanks for coming tonight."

"As if I'd miss a free dinner at Carter's. I hope one of the guys from *The Burnt Clovers* are in town. They're really blowing up and the last time my sorority sister Kelsey dined there, she met Derek Reiner. Can you believe that? She said…"

I half listen as Carmen rattles on and on about the best band to come out of Boston this decade. Will Abbi and Aiden already be cuddled up by the time we arrive? Will she be furious with me for showing up at Carter's? Will she let Aiden kiss her?

These thoughts plague my mind until I valet at Carter's, both impressed and annoyed that Carmen is still chattering about Derek Reiner, lead singer for *The Burnt Clovers*.

"Pandatelli. For two," I tell the hostess as she escorts us to our table.

The entire time, my eyes scan the restaurant for a sign of Abbi. I spot her and Aiden talking animatedly about four tables over from where Carmen and I are seated.

I slip into my chair and pick up a menu, glancing over the top to keep an eye on Abbi. I frown, pressure building in my chest. She looks at ease around Aiden. Her eyes are bright and shining, her hands flying as she says something that makes him chuckle and lean forward in his seat. Their server drops off a bottle of wine and my stomach drops.

"…to drink?" Carmen asks.

"Huh?" I look at her.

"I'm thinking one of their signature cocktails. I promise I won't puke in your car this time."

I chuckle. "I'll just grab a beer."

"Stop staring so hard," Carmen advises. "You look desperate."

"I feel desperate," I admit. Abbi looks gorgeous. Effortless. Even though I saw her an hour ago in a smelly high school gym, rocking the same black pants and silk blouse, in the environment of Carter's, her demeanor has changed. Or is it because of *him*?

They cheers and I grip the underside of the table to keep myself rooted in my chair when I really want to vault myself over the table and claim Abbi the same way I did in July. Completely.

"Are you ready to order?" Our server appears.

Carmen rattles off her meal choice and I order a steak with potatoes and a Caesar salad.

I have no idea what the hell transpires over dinner. I keep one ear tuned into Carmen as she talks about her first week of classes, her family back home, and her sorority. Soon, her attention is snagged by a few well-known athletes dining at a back table and she whips out her phone to text her sorority sister, completely enthralled. I can relate, since I can't tear my gaze from Abbi.

At one point, Abbi takes a sip of her wine, her fingers toying with the ends of her hair. It's as if she can feel my gaze because she turns and our eyes connect. Hold. Hers widen, surprised before they narrow in...hurt? Anger? Disbelief?

Her gaze flickers to Carmen and an emotion I can't name ripples over her face. The fact that she felt *something* gives me a glimmer of hope before Carmen murmurs across the table.

"What?" I ask her.

"She's pissed at you," Carmen explains, shaking her head. "And honestly, I would be too. Couldn't you get one of your guy friends to come to dinner tonight?"

I remain silent, knowing that yeah, I could have. But I *wanted* to make Abbi jealous because I've been nothing but green with envy since she moved to Boston.

Carmen clucks her tongue. "You're an idiot."

Shit. By the way Abbi actively refuses to look in my direction for the rest of dinner, I know Carmen is right. I messed this up big time by letting my anger and jealousy fuel my actions. Now, I'm forced to watch as Abbi shamelessly flirts with Aiden, the two of their heads bent together like they've been dating for weeks and not mere minutes.

She likes him. I can tell by the way she smiles at him, laughs when he says something funny. I can tell by the way she avoids glancing in my direction of the room for the rest of the evening. When Aiden settles his bill, I ask for mine.

When he pulls out Abbi's chair, I alert Carmen to the fact that we're wrapping things up.

"Good, because this is starting to get awkward," she responds.

"Thanks for coming tonight."

"Panda, if you like this girl so much, why not just talk to her?" Carmen asks the obvious question.

"Because I'm an idiot," I remind her.

"Well, you better smarten up because there's no way in hell a girl like that"—Carmen flicks her fingers toward Abbi's empty table—"will give this"—she taps a fingernail against our table top—"a real chance. She looks way too put together to put up with your head games."

I swear softly and nod, knowing Carmen is right. I punch her lightly on the shoulder. "Thanks for the wisdom, kid."

"Anytime. You and my brother are seriously clueless when it comes to women."

I'm forced to agree as I watch Aiden's fingers press into the small of Abbi's back as he guides her toward the exit. He hovers over her shoulder and she smiles up at him like he hung the fucking moon instead of bought her a steak.

A desperate need to fix this, fix everything between Abbi and me, grips me. Carmen was right; I need to talk to her. I need to tell her that shutting her down was a massive mistake, one that I've regretted ever since she returned to Boston. I need to apologize for hurting her. Tonight. Now. Suddenly, it feels like I've run out of time and if I don't see Abbi tonight, I'll lose her forever.

The only good bit of fortune is that I messaged Torsten Hansen for Abbi's address, under the bullshit lie that she needed help moving some furniture. So, sue me, okay? The important thing is that after I drop Carmen off at home, I head toward Abbi's place.

I lope into the building, waving to reception as I pass. In a matter of seconds, I'm in the elevator, riding up to the four-teenth floor. My heart hammers in my head as nerves, excitement, and a healthy dose of fear shoot through me. Did she invite Aiden back to her place? Is she even home? Did she kiss him good night? Worse, are they…intimately together right now?

The thought makes me want to puke and I bang on the door with more force then necessary.

It swings wide open. Abbi stands on the other side of the threshold, an oversized sweater hanging off one shoulder, glaring at me. Her chest heaves with deep, angry breaths, and her face is red.

Is she crying?

I shuffle forward, my arm outstretched.

She swats my hand away and snarls, "I hate you, Luca Pandatelli."

CHAPTER 7
ABBI

I glare at Luca, my anger rushing forth like a tsunami. "How dare you crash my date with Aiden? Why were you at Carter's? Why are you doing this to me?" I turn away from him and stride into my living room, both wanting him to leave and to follow me inside.

Jesus, what is wrong with me? Why can't I slam the door in his face?

Hurt blares to the forefront of my mind but desire pools low in my stomach and I hate my stupid body for reacting to Luca when my head, no my heart, knows better than to trust whatever the hell comes out of his mouth.

"Is he here?" Luca shuts the door behind me and I feel his presence enter my space, overwhelming it as easily as he overwhelms me. "Did he hurt you?"

I spin around, disbelief causing my mouth to drop open. "Why would you even think that?"

Luca's eyes are narrowed, his teeth clenched. "You're crying." His words are soft, at odds with the ferocity in his expression.

I cover my face with my hand, trying to calm down with a breathing exercise my therapist recommended after my mom passed. I've spent the better part of my life in therapy and still, I'm a hurricane of emotions, too much hurt and not enough logic.

Luca steps closer and his hands tentatively settle on my shoulders. "Abbi," his voice is pained and it makes me squeeze my eyes closed.

"Why are you doing this to me?" I groan out, too upset to care at how obvious I'm being. *I hate him*, I remind myself.

My inner self cracks up, slapping her knee. *Yeah, right.*

"Doing what?" he asks, surprised.

Gently, he pulls my hand away from my face. The concern in his eyes obliterates the wall I've been wrapping around my heart since the last time he rejected me.

"You never called," I accuse him.

Shame fills the lines of his face and he dips his head in acknowledgement.

"I thought that weekend…" I trail off.

"Abbi…" His voice is tortured. But what does it *mean*? "That weekend…" His voice cracks and he closes his eyes.

I stand perfectly still, waiting, as hope swirls in a flurry around me.

"What happened with Phil?" he murmurs.

I let out the most unattractive sound I've heard and turn away. "Phil turned out to be a disaster. Maybe the biggest mistake I've made in a long line of fuckups."

"What happened?" He's close behind me, trailing me into the kitchen.

I reach into my fridge and pull out a couple of White Claws. I offer him one and he accepts it wordlessly, popping the tab and taking a swig.

I sigh. "Did you know my gran passed?"

His eyes flash, his Adam's apple bobbing once. "No." The word scrapes at the air between us, thick and clumsy.

"Well, it's just me now." I hold my arms out to the side before letting them fall. "I can't keep doing this, Luca."

"Doing what?"

"Setting myself up for disappointment."

His brow furrows and he shuffles closer.

"I believed you. I *trusted* you. I thought that weekend meant something and when you didn't call…it hurt, okay? It hurt more than it should have and it hurt more than I wanted to admit."

"Fuck, Abbi. I'm so fucking sorry." His words are laced with regret. "That weekend meant something. It was everything."

Shock rolls through me as I narrow my eyes. Is he serious? At the sincerity in his tone and the ferocity in his expression, I shake my head. My hand wraps around the base of my throat as I whisper, "Then why didn't you call?"

He moves closer. "Right after you left, my sister called. My pop had a heart attack—"

"Shit," I swear, feeling like it.

"No, no he's okay."

"Really?"

"Yeah." Luca nods. "But the rest of the summer was a whirlwind. I spent most of it in Philly. My family…they're my life, Abbi. When they need me, I show up and kind of forget about everything else. By the time I got back to Boston and the dust settled, it was too late to call. I figured you've moved on with your life and that weekend was sort of this fun reminder of summer. Besides, I told you not to settle and that's exactly what you'd be doing with me. My family needs me now, more than ever before, and I'm never around. Every chance I get, I'm flying down to Philly."

I nod slowly, his words making sense even if they're painful to hear. But his dad had a heart attack… I wrack my mind, vaguely recalling Chloe bringing Luca up but me shutting her down. At the time, I was in the thick of things with Phil and losing my job. The mention of Luca was another piece of poop in a raging shitstorm.

"Do you like Aiden?" he asks.

I nod. I bet every person Aiden's ever met likes him. He's a likable guy; definitely in the friend zone, but still, likable.

"Are you going to go out with him again?"

I stare at Luca for a long time, wishing I could rewind to July. Would I have been more honest with him then? Would it have mattered?

"Why did you show up at Carter's with that blonde girl?" I ask instead of responding. The truth is, Aiden and I had a great time. And we both knew about three minutes into our date that there wasn't any chemistry between us. In a weird way, it was this big relief. We laughed really hard, agreed to be friends, and had an animated conversation and a great meal. Aiden moved to the city about a year ago and promised to introduce me to new friends of his and even mentioned setting me up if I'm really on the hunt.

Apparently, things with one of his colleagues is a complicated mess and I can relate because…exhibit A.

"Because I was jealous. And I wanted to make you jealous," Luca says honestly, dipping his head so his eyes can hold mine. "Carmen is my college teammate's kid sister. She's pretty much become my kid sister since she started at Boston College a few years ago. And to be honest with you, she's less than impressed with me right now and thinks I need to man up and talk to you."

I snort, my jealousy over the young, beautiful blonde easing. "Smart girl."

"Were you?" Luca asks.

I frown. "Jealous?"

He nods.

I roll my eyes and swat at him. "What do you think?"

He smirks and wraps his arms around my waist, pulling me closer. I let him, sinking into his embrace. And God, does it feel good. His arms around me cause a ripple of goosebumps to dance over my skin, a thrill to flare through my limbs, and desire to pool in my stomach. My body, traitor that it is, remembers every sensation he pulled from it more than six months ago and it wants it again.

I want him again. I shake my head. "We work together."

"Not really."

"I don't trust you," I revise.

"I know." His response is quiet but he doesn't drop his hold. "Are you going out with him again?"

I widen my eyes, annoyed and excited. I need to get my head examined. This is why I end up in these situations. I'm too rash. Too much wanting and not enough thinking.

"We're friends."

"You looked like more than that."

"You looked like you were on a date with a college sorority girl," I point out.

Luca wrinkles his nose as if the thought offends him. "Well, I wasn't. I don't know what the hell I was trying to do except see you. And right now, I'm here, Abbi." His hand presses in the center of my back.

I shrug. I should shake off his touch. But I *can't*.

"Luca, I can't handle any more hurt. I've had a lifetime of it and I'm…I'm tired."

"Me too," he murmurs back, his hand cupping my cheek. He angles my head and looks me over like he's committing me to memory—every eyelash, the curve of my lips, the slope of my nose. "I've made a lot of mistakes, Abbi Walsh. But one of the biggest was hurting you."

I glance at his mouth, his lips moving to speak the words I waited months to hear. Is it too late? Can I give him another chance?

What the hell happened to professional, polite, and detached?

Luca's hand slips higher on my back.

I look up, feeling my eyes widen at the naked desire in his expression.

Is that all this is? Desire? Want? Messy feelings and complicated motives? How can I trust his truth when last time, he didn't follow through?

His mouth arcs closer to mine.

"Wait." My palm presses into his chest and he freezes. "What's changed?"

"What?"

"What's different now? You admitted you're here because you're jealous."

"So?" he growls.

"So, if you didn't see me out with Aiden, would you have knocked on my door?"

Luca sighs and stares at me. I lift an eyebrow, waiting. The longer he hesitates, the faster my stomach falls.

His phone rings and he swears, turning away from me and pulling it from his pocket.

"Hey," he answers.

The temperature between us, skyrocketing moments ago, turns glacial. Bitterness climbs up my throat like ivy, snaking around my wagging tongue, making it immobile.

"Valentina?" he murmurs and my heart aches. "When?"

Oh, God, how stupid can a person feel?

"Yeah, I'll be there. Of course, I will. Yeah. 'Bye." He slips his phone back into his pocket.

When he turns, his expression falls at whatever he reads on my face. "Abbi, that was—"

"You need to go," I cut him off, not wanting to hear any more bullshit.

His forehead crinkles and his eyes harden. "Are you kidding me right now?"

"Me?" I jab my finger into my chest and wince. "Why don't you ask yourself that question, Panda?"

He shakes his head, scoffing. "Wow. We're back to that again? Abbi, I thought we were moving forward."

"Funny." I blow past him, yanking open my apartment

door. "I thought so too. Thanks for reminding me why this is such a bad idea."

I don't make eye contact as he stalks past me. Once he clears the space, I slam the door behind him.

Then, I walk back into my bedroom, throw myself down on my bed, and scream into my pillow. Tears tumble down my cheeks as I sob, desperately missing my gran and the advice she would surely share if she was here. When I've calmed down a bit, I pull out the last letter she wrote me. God, I wish she was here. I wish I could feel close to her again.

Her handwriting makes me smile. Her letter is replete with wisdom and advice. It's written with humor and love. It's the last thing I have from the woman who raised me.

When I fold it up and tuck it back into my nightstand drawer, all I'm left with is overwhelming sadness. For a woman who seems to have it all together, I sure as hell have nothing worth holding on to.

CHAPTER 8
LUCA

What the hell did I do? Does Abbi truly think so little of me that she believes I'd take a call from another woman while standing in her apartment, apologizing to her? Shit, she wasn't kidding when she said she doesn't trust me.

But how am I supposed to earn her trust if she won't hear me out? Why can't I seem to make headway with her? The things she confided in me about her father and past relationships roll through my mind and dread settles in my stomach. Did my not calling hurt her the same way they did? Is she grouping me in with the other men who came before me? The un-fucking-worthy ones? And why didn't I make the connection sooner?

A few inches of snow coats the ground as I slowly pull into my parking garage. I make my way up to my condo, the exhaustion I've kept at bay all day rising to meet me.

My phone rings again and I swear, my irritation turning to guilt, as my niece Laura's name flashes across the screen.

I frown. Why is Laura, only nine years old, calling so late?

"Laur?" I answer.

She sniffles through the line and my heart breaks. "Hi, Uncle Luca."

"What's going on, ladybug?" I ask, dropping into a chair in my living room.

"Can't sleep."

"Another bad dream?"

"Yeah." Her voice is tiny and I wish I was there to hug her.

"Where's your mama and brothers?"

"I don't want to wake them."

I chuckle, my frustration over messing things up with Abbi again receding as I focus on my niece.

"Can you tell me a story?" she asks.

"Of course," I say as an old memory of Laura's parents at the beach, the Jersey shore, comes to mind. I settle deeper into my chair and start, "It was Fourth of July weekend and…"

I wake up the next morning with a stiff neck, a dry mouth, and a cramp in my leg. Fuck. I slept in a goddamn armchair.

I squint at the time. 9:38 a.m.

JUSTINE

Thanks for putting my kid to sleep last night.

I glance out the living room windows and grin as snow blankets the city streets.

Letting out a laugh, I relocate to the window like a little kid on Christmas morning. I've always loved winter. There's something magical about snow, something that pulls me back to my childhood and good, happy memories. Moments with my mom. She used to have a big, red mug that she would make hot chocolate in instead of coffee.

I press my fingertips against the cold windowpane as if I could reach out and grip a piece of my childhood. Nostalgia washes over me and for a second, I wish I lived back in Philadelphia. On a day like today, I'd round up my nieces and nephews and take them sledding. Robbie and Pop would be out plowing for extra money. Jenni would bake chocolate chip cookies and hum to classic rock songs. I can picture it perfectly and I suddenly wish it was possible.

The shrill ring of my phone interrupts that silly daydream. I blow out a sigh and lift my phone to look at the screen.

When I read Chloe's name, I frown. Why is she calling me?

I pick up. "Hey, Chlo."

"Panda. Oh, good. You're home. Wait, are you home?" she asks.

"Yeah," I say slowly. "Are you okay? All good with Cap?"

"Yeah, yeah. It's not me…it's Abbi."

"Abbi?" Concern rushes through me.

"I wouldn't call you if Austin was home. But he went to help his parents shovel out this morning and—"

"What happened?"

Chloe sighs. "She's going to kill me for telling you but—"

"Chloe," I press her.

"She thinks she needs stitches."

"Stitches! What the hell happened?"

"Um…she fell. In the shower. And, uh, she hit her face."

I'm already pulling on my winter coat and grabbing my keys. "I'm on my way over."

Chloe breathes out a grateful sigh. "Thank you, Panda. You're the only person close enough to walk. I just, I'm worried about her and she's new to the city and—"

"Don't worry about it. I'm on my way," I say, stepping out into the cold morning.

Abbi's building is only two down from mine but since we're situated on the water, the wind is cutting, slashing against my face and kicking up snow, so the walk takes longer than I'd like.

When I'm finally inside the elevator, on my way up to her floor, I take off my coat and shake out the snow. I knock on her door and listen carefully for her footsteps.

A moment later, she opens it the smallest bit, peeking out at me.

"I can't believe she called you," she murmurs.

"Open up," I say instead.

She does and I slip inside, closing the door behind me. Then I turn around and take her in, wincing at the wadded-up paper towels she has pressed against her left eyebrow.

"How'd you fall?" I ask, touching her wrist and leading her to the couch. I push her into the seat and hover over her, gentle not to hurt her.

"Fell in the shower," she admits sheepishly, the deep V of her robe opening as she hunches forward.

"Lean back, Abs. Let me take a look," I say, guiding her back into the cushions.

When she acquiesces, I place my hand on top of hers and slowly shift the paper towels away. I wince at the gash cutting through her eyebrow. Immediately, dark red blood pools up. I look closely, biting my lip. "It's pretty deep."

"Do you think I need stitches?"

I touch around the injury gently. "I don't think so…"

"Okay."

"I brought glue." I place the wadded-up paper towel back in place.

"Glue?" Horror threads through her tone and I try not to smile.

"It's skin glue. For injuries," I explain.

"Oh."

"If you want to head to the ER, I'll take you. But I don't think it's deep enough for stitches and you'll be waiting hours."

"No, it's okay. It's pretty much blizzarding out. We can try the glue."

"'Kay." I swing a leg over her lap, essentially straddling her.

"What are you doing?" she asks, her voice deeper than it was a moment ago.

I fight my smile. "Working." I pull a packet of an antiseptic wipe and the glue from my back pocket. I glance down at her, noting the pretty blush on her cheeks. God, she's beautiful. To think I once kissed those luscious lips. To think I once traced her curves and felt her moving beneath me.

"Luca."

"Right. Hold still, okay?"

"Okay," she whispers, her eyes wide.

I settle more firmly over her, clean her wound, and set to work, careful to create as straight a fusion as possible. Abbi doesn't move beneath me. With the exception of one sharp inhale of breath, one wouldn't think she was even conscious.

When I'm done, I pull back to study my work. "You may have a small scar."

"That's the least of my problems."

I slip off her and settle next to her on the couch, taking the bloody paper towel from her hand and closing it in my fist. "What are your problems, Abbi Walsh?"

She smirks and shakes her head. "Thank you for coming, Luca. You, well, you didn't have to." She takes in my sweater and jeans pointedly.

"What's that look for?" I wonder aloud.

Her eyes scan my body slowly before she rolls them. "Clearly, you were busy and Chloe interrupted you when she called."

I frown. What the hell is she talking about? I glance down at my sweater and then I start laughing. "Wait, you think I was—" My own laughter cuts off my words.

Abbi frowns at me, narrowing her eyes. With her messed-up eyebrow, she looks tough, almost menacing, and the visual makes me laugh harder.

"I went home last night and passed out," I say. When she doesn't look convinced, I add, "My niece called me because she couldn't sleep. I sat down to tell her a story and…woke up this morning to a winter wonderland and a crick in my neck."

At that, some of the skepticism in her eyes fades and she almost smiles. "You want a coffee?"

I nod. "I'd love one."

"Okay." She stands up but sways on her feet.

"Whoa," I say, my hand darting out to grab her wrist. I ease her back down. "You fell pretty hard, huh?"

She rolls her lips and blows out a sigh. "I tripped over the ledge getting out of the shower and smacked my face against the vanity. I'm fine. I just, stood up too fast."

I watch her closely, noting the flush that works its way up from her chest, fanning out over her cheeks.

"Slow this time," I caution, placing my hands under her elbows and helping her stand.

"I'm really okay," she says but it's more of a whisper, as if she's trying to convince herself.

"Of course you are."

Her eyes meet mine and hold, some of the wariness fading away. "Thank you for coming."

"I'm here for you, Abbi."

Her nostrils flare but she doesn't respond. Instead, she walks to the kitchen and I follow, trying not to imagine how easily her robe could slip from her shoulders.

Is she wearing lace panties underneath? Or bare?

My cock hardens from the thought, either of them, and I suddenly wish I kissed her last night. If Nikki hadn't called, would I have made a move? Would she have reciprocated?

Will she give me another shot to see if we can be more than a series of hypothetical questions?

I hope so.

CHAPTER 9
ABBI

P lows roam up and down the streets, clearing snow and spraying salt. The sky is gray and overcast and the wind howls as it whips past my windows.

But inside, it's cozy and warm. The center of my kitchen table is set with a tray of candles, all lit and giving off delicious wintery scents. I'm wearing my favorite oversized sweater and leggings. My feet are wrapped in plush slippers and my hand is wrapped around an oversized mug of coffee.

I settle into the corner of the couch, close my eyes, and take a deep breath.

"You need anything?" Luca asks, his voice causing my nerves to tingle.

I need a lot of things. Luckily, I don't voice the thought. I open my eyes to see him standing uncertainly on the edge of the living room, hovering like he isn't sure if he should stay or go. Well, that makes two of us.

The least I can do is offer to make him breakfast. After he dropped everything to come to my aid and then I insinuated that he had a one-night stand…

"Abs?" He clears his throat.

I blush and dip my head, taking a large gulp of coffee. The

mug I brought into the living room for Luca while he was in the bathroom rests, untouched, on the coffee table.

"Want to have some coffee?" I lift my chin in the direction of the mug. "I can make us breakfast."

"You don't have to do that," he says but he rounds the chair and settles into it, bringing the coffee mug with him. He takes a sip and sighs appreciatively, his own eyes closing for a moment.

"You look tired," I comment.

His eyes pop open. Well, it wasn't the nicest thing to say but it was truthful.

"I've been busy lately," he murmurs. "A lot of flying."

"How are they doing?" I ask, wanting to know more about his family dynamics, about the way he's stepping up for the people he loves most.

"Okay. It's just…a lot sometimes…with Pop. My sisters." He clears his throat. "I should get going." He moves to stand and my heart flutters, not ready for him to leave even though logic should dictate that I push him through the door. I feel shaky, uneasy. Partially from the images Phil sent me this morning that led to my bathroom stumble and partially from Luca's presence. Not only do I not want Luca to leave; I want to sit here and listen to him talk about his family. I want him to give me more pieces of himself, to remind me that there are good men in the world, specifically in the wake of Phil's latest messages.

"Don't," I murmur. "Let me make breakfast. It's the least I can do." I stand and move toward the kitchen.

Luca hesitates, his eyes studying mine with an intensity that confuses me. "I'm not a bad guy," he says finally.

"I know that." I do. Deep down, my heart even knows that Luca is one of the good ones.

He reaches for my arm, his fingers linking around my wrist. He tugs gently, until I turn and look up at him. "I know

I hurt you and I'm so fucking sorry, Abbi. But you can trust me. You can talk to me."

I scoff and roll my eyes, but I'm touched by the sincerity in his tone. In fact, his words, the seriousness in his eyes when he says them, sends a ripple of pleasure through me, straight to the place between my thighs that is desperate for him. Jesus, I'm losing it. "Are you a bacon and eggs guy? Or do you prefer pancakes?"

The corner of Luca's mouth twitches, calling me out on my deflection. But he doesn't voice it. He just drops my wrist and says, "Bacon and eggs."

I nod and walk into the kitchen. I pour a second mug of coffee, which probably isn't the best idea since I already feel jittery. I pull the necessary ingredients out of the refrigerator and get to work, keenly aware of Luca perched on the edge of a barstool.

My body tightens under his gaze. Why the hell does he have to look like one of those sexy, too perfect men that grace the covers of romance novels? Men like that aren't supposed to exist in real life. Yet, I can't tear my eyes away from the way Luca traces the rim of his coffee mug. His finger slow and steady, his lips pursed in thought.

I force my eyes to the stove, to the frying pan, to making breakfast. This shouldn't feel seductive. Cooking breakfast for a man shouldn't feel thrilling or daring. It should feel like drudgery.

As the oil heats up in the pan, the temperature in the room jumps. My skin heats, my stomach tightening. The sizzle of bacon fills the air. I crack the eggs, whisking them furiously as I feel Luca's eyes on me, centered in the space between my shoulder blades.

Will it always be like this? An irrefutable connection? A chemistry that sparks?

Why can't I ever like the safe, boring men that Chloe

suggested? Why couldn't I feel a zing with a nice guy, a man like Aiden?

Just when I think I can shut Luca out, he does something to reel me in. He shows up. He offers his help. He shoots me a smile that makes me feel like I'm flying. He proves that he's nothing like Phil. Or Kent. Or my father. And my heart softens the slightest bit toward him.

My emotions wreak havoc on my body and suddenly, I feel like sobbing. I feel like dropping to my knees and crying until my hurt drains out, until my fear over Phil's subtle threats disappear, until I can think of Gran and smile.

Luca's hand appears on my hip, his other hand covering mine and squeezing until I stop whisking. His chest, hard and strong, shadows my back. I hear his sharp inhale and a flood of tears rushes forward, filling my eyes with humiliation, heartache, and a desperate kind of longing.

Luca takes the bowl from my hand and places it on the countertop with a thud. Then he turns me in his arms, stepping forward until I'm pinned between him and the counter, with nowhere to look but up. His eyes overflow with confusion and regret.

My tears spill over, a few tracking my cheeks with a slowness that is movie-worthy.

Luca takes in my tears and his jaw clenches. He lifts his hand slowly and brushes his fingers over my cheeks as one might a child. "Talk to me, Abbi."

At the genuine concern in his voice, my face crumples. I lean forward, dropping my forehead against his chest. I hear him turn the stove off before he wraps his arms around me, holding me in an embrace that feels like a safety net when it should feel like a danger zone.

"Abbi," Luca murmurs, his fingers lacing through my hair, his hand steady in the center of my back.

I take a deep breath, my tears wetting the front of his shirt. I breathe him in, winter and aftershave and man, and the scent is soothing. I'm not sure how long I stand wrapped up in Luca but eventually, he shifts. He pulls back slightly, his hand cups my cheek and angles my face up toward his.

What I read in his expression undoes me. Anguish lines his face and pain rings his eyes. "Please, confide in me, sweet girl."

I roll my lips together and fall into the pools of his eyes. His hands rub up and down the sides of my body, comforting.

He tips forward and kisses my forehead, lingering long enough for my eyes to drop, for me to savor the moment, somehow knowing it means more than this instant. "I'm making breakfast. Go sit down."

"You don't have to—" My voice sounds strangled.

"Please. Let me do this for you. Let me in." His tone holds a note of pleading that I *want* to trust.

I nod and slip onto the barstool he vacated. Staring at his back, I watch him flip on the stove to finish cooking our bacon before pouring in the egg mixture. He moves around my kitchen like he's been in it before.

When he slides a plate piled with bacon, eggs, and toast in front of me, my emotional outburst has quieted. Embarrassment wraps around me but not to the degree of humiliation one would expect. Instead, I mostly feel relieved. I've been holding so much inside for so long and it felt good, cathartic even, to release some of the buildup.

Luca slips onto the barstool beside me. "What's going on, baby?" he tries again, the endearment sliding off his tongue like he says it to me all the time.

I take a deep breath, about to shoot back something lighthearted but a piece of the truth tumbles out instead. "My gran died."

His hand covers mine. "I know. And I hate that you're hurting so badly, Abbi."

"I lost my job," I add and his eyes narrow.

"When?"

"November." My fingers tap the end of my fork, nervousness racing through me.

"Phil?" he asks, the word holding more meaning than the name alone.

I nod, cringing as the images on my phone blare in my mind. "Turns out he was married. And I'm the home-wrecking slut that—"

"Don't talk about yourself like that," Luca cuts me off, anger sharp in his voice.

I sigh. "Boston is supposed to be my fresh start," I explain, forcing myself to meet his eyes.

"But it means having me in your life," he surmises.

"You didn't call." I wish I don't sound so brokenhearted when I say it but maybe it's for the best. Maybe this therapy session is going to be a turning point. Maybe I'm finally moving forward with my life, shedding some of the emotional baggage I carry around like a cargo plane.

"I wish I did."

My eyes widen at the admission.

Luca shifts in his seat, spinning both of us so we're facing each other, my knees tucked in between his, my hands clasped in his. "I've never done this before, Abbi."

"Blown a girl off?"

The corner of his mouth lifts. "No smartass. I've never tried before. Usually, women flock to me and I—"

"I get it."

He chuckles. "You scare me."

I roll my eyes. "I scare you?"

Luca bites his bottom lip and the air between us tightens. "The way I feel about you, how much I feel for you, scares me," he admits.

What. The. Hell.

My mouth drops open and his eyes lighten, zeroing in on my lips.

"Weren't expecting that bit of truth, huh?" he teases.

I shake my head. Luca's hand falls to the side of my thigh, splaying widely.

"I like you, Abbi Walsh. I care about you. I want to be here for you. I know I fucked everything up over the summer but…shit…" He pauses, scratching his cheek. "This is going to sound cliché as fuck but I've grown up a lot. Things with my family…"

"It's been real."

"Really intense."

"You're overwhelmed."

"Buried," he admits. "You're like a snowflake in the middle of a Nor'easter."

I snort, raising my eyebrows. "I don't know what the means."

"Means your special, Abbi. Means when I look at you, I see this one, singular, unique person in the midst of so much fucking chaos. I don't know how to protect you from the disaster of my life. I don't know how to be here the way you need me to be. I want to show up for you but I'm up to my eyeballs in—"

"Snowbanks," I murmur.

He smiles but it's sad. "It's not going to melt anytime soon. My family is…a lot. I have two sisters and two brothers. My youngest brother is in the military, living in Texas. The rest of my family are in Philly. I've got a bunch of nieces and nephews. Both of my brothers-in-law are no longer in the picture, for different reasons, so I help out a lot."

"Like telling bedtime stories?"

"I do all the characters' voices."

I grin because I can picture it perfectly. "You're the fun uncle."

"Of course," he says, almost sounding offended. "I love my family but it also means that there's not as much time for my own life."

"I know what you mean," I say softly. "For years, I was Gran's sole caregiver. Then, when I moved her into the nursing home, I was her financial and emotional support." I meet Luca's understanding eyes. "Not that Gran held me back because I wanted to be there for her, but she did weigh heavily on my conscience."

"I get it. You wanted to put her first so sometimes, decisions were made for you. But they may not have been the decisions you would have made if things were different."

"Exactly. I never would have moved here if she was still alive."

Luca's touch is soft on my arm. "I'm sorry you're hurting, Abs. I hate seeing you drown in pain."

"I just miss her."

"I know."

"I always wondered what it would be like to have a big family," I say.

Luca dips his head. "It's chaos. Wildness. But it's fun too. I never imagined what it would be like to not have my siblings."

"It's lonely," I share. "Isolating."

Luca reaches out and brushes my hair back from my face, careful not to touch the gash on my forehead. "Give me a shot, Abbi. I swear I'll never let you be lonely again."

I shake my head, knowing that's not a promise he can make. No one can. "It's not like that. I can be in a room full of people and still feel lonely…"

His eyebrows draw together. "How?"

I shrug. "Been on my own too long. I don't know how, I can't, connect sometimes."

"You connect perfectly with me."

I laugh. "Yeah, the sex was really hot."

He smirks but his eyes remain serious, unwilling to take the levity I offered. "Wasn't talking about connecting in bed, Abbi."

I swallow thickly. "I'm not like the women you're usually with."

"You're the first woman I've ever really been with."

The rapid beating of my heart starts to overtake the logic I swore I'd stick to.

"You're the first one who's meant more than a moment, Abbi. A hell of a lot more."

My fingertips tingle and I draw in a shaky inhale.

"You can trust me, baby. Trust the fact that I never do anything like this." He gestures in between us and to the kitchen at large. "With the exception of the women in my family, I don't go out of my way for women at all. But I want to be here for you. Let me."

I hold his eyes for a long moment, weighing his words with his expression. My heart races and I feel like laughing and vomiting.

Take a leap of faith, Abigail. Gran's voice fills my head as clear as if she was sitting next to me.

"Yes."

Luca smiles like I just announced he was inducted into the Hockey Hall of Fame. His entire face brightens, his eyes spark, and a satisfaction I've never known rolls through me.

"Yes," he repeats.

Then, he leans forward and captures my lips in a kiss that flips my world upside down. All I can focus on is him, the feel of his mouth against mine, the beat of his heart underneath my palm.

Luca slams through some of my walls as I dent some of the steel in his coat of armor. It isn't a perfect combination, but Luca is right. It's more of a connection than I've ever experienced before.

It's a connection that counts, one that both thrills and terrifies me.

CHAPTER 10
LUCA

My legs burn as I sprint the last hundred meters. Sweat courses down my back, causing my T-shirt to stick to my skin, settling into the waistband of my joggers. The faces I fly past stare at me with a mix of awe and surprise that motivates me to move faster.

My arms pump furiously. The sound of my sneakers pounding the pavement, my own heartbeat, my measured breathing, are the only sounds I latch onto.

Go, move, faster, Pandatelli.

When I reach the front of my building, I ease into a jog. By the time I reach the next corner, I slow to a walk. I breathe out and raise my hands to the back of my head.

Exhaling, my breath creates a puff of smoke in the cold, early morning air. I half-heartedly go through a quick stretching routine, my mind still racing despite the tough run.

A lot of people think that just because I stand in a net, I don't need to condition the way the other guys on the team do. But that's bullshit. I may not fly up the ice on a breakaway the way East does or skate backwards as easily as I breathe like James, but I need to be agile as fuck to contort my body and block shots.

Today's run was on another level. It was more than my normal workout routine dictates. This morning, I ran for mental clarity and as I lean forward, my hands gripping my kneecaps as I suck in a deep inhale, it did jack shit.

Because images of Abbi still play on a loop in my mind. The scent of her hair still sticks to my skin and the feel of her curves still cause my fingers to twitch. Kissing Abbi shouldn't be a novelty in my life; Lord knows I'm not a saint. But with her, something changed. In one instant, my world flipped and the frustration and anger I've been carrying around for weeks became lighter. Hopeful. Desirous as hell.

For the first time in my life, I don't know how to play it. With women, I'm charming. I do casual, fun, live-in-the-moment carelessness. But now I've got the woman of my dreams, of any man's dreams, as *mine*. It's as gratifying as it is terrifying. How the hell can I do this without mucking it all up?

Will my past bother her? Will my family obligations be too much? Will we even want the same things in a few months from now? How the hell does all of this work?

I straighten my back and look up at Abbi's building which I just happened to find myself standing in front of. Obviously, it wasn't a planned-out thing. We're practically neighbors.

Do I call her? Is that too forward?

I growl at myself for being so inept at this. Most guys know how to date by the time they're in their thirties. Instead, I feel like a bumbling high schooler with too much testosterone and not enough common sense.

The wind whips around me and as my sweat begins to dry, the cold starts to seep into my bones. All right, enough of this. Game time decision. I told Abbi I was all in and that means committing. It also means communicating.

I slip my phone out of my pocket and dial her number.

"Hello?" she answers, sleep and surprise in her voice.

It makes me smile and now I'm the loser standing outside

her building, peering up at it as if I know which window is hers (I don't), and grinning like I just won an award. I take a breath, a chuckle working its way up my throat at how lame I am. "Morning, Abs."

"Good morning, Luca." I can hear the smile in her voice too and it emboldens me to continue.

"Sleep well?"

"Uh-huh. You?"

"Very."

"Good."

"Good."

A few seconds of silence tick by and while it should feel awkward, it doesn't. I laugh lightly and blurt out, "I just finished my run. I'm standing in front of your building freezing my balls off, trying to work up the courage to invite you to breakfast."

She laughs and the sound warms me from the inside out. Who needs a winter coat and a scarf when you can listen to pure sunshine?

"Would you like to come up?" she asks, a layer of sexiness to her tone. I open my mouth but she adds, "I don't want your balls to freeze off. I kind of like them."

A shot of laughter bursts from my lips. "I'm coming up now."

"See you in a second." She disconnects and I shake my head, entering her building.

The heat hits me full blast and I realize how disgusting I am. Sweaty, stinky, and definitely not the way a boyfriend should show up at his girlfriend's door. That thought makes me freeze in front of the elevators.

Is that what I am? A boyfriend?

The word feels strange as I test it out. Not bad, just different.

When the elevator doors open, I step inside and note in

the mirror that I'm smiling again. Yeah, I can be Abbi's boyfriend. I *want* to be Abbi's boyfriend.

No more fucking Phils or Aidens for her. From here on out, she's mine and I'm going to be here for her. I'm going to do every damn thing I can to prove that to her.

By the time she answers her door, my nerves have dissipated. My second-guessing is gone. I'm left with her beaming face and my desire to kiss it. So, I do.

Being with Abbi feels right, the same way playing hockey does. I'm going to trust that.

"Morning." I kiss her again.

"You said that already."

"You hungry?" I step inside, my eyes dropping down the length of her body. How the hell a girl can make leggings and a flannel sexy is beyond me but Abbi is rocking the shit out of this blue-and-green plaid like a Scottish bride.

She nods slowly, her eyes drinking me in like she's thirsty.

I bite the corner of my mouth and her eyes widen. I lunge for her and she laughs, her arms automatically encircling my neck as I hitch her into my arms. Her lean legs wrap around my waist and I catch the ends of her hair, tipping her face up so I can kiss her full-on.

Our lips meet hastily, our teeth clashing. She snorts and I chuckle and then I'm kissing her the way I thought about every damn day for the past six months. Thoroughly and completely.

I move toward the kitchen, depositing Abbi on her kitchen table. Her legs widen and I step between them, my palm planting in the space beside her hip. I lean forward, her hands grip the front of my hoodie, and we *kiss*. It's intense, the feel of her lips over mine. It's sexy, the slip of her tongue against mine. It's hot, the sounds of her need mixing with mine. I slant my mouth over hers, my other hand wrapping around her waist to hold her against me as I deepen our connection.

Desire races through my blood as I harden for her. I lean

her back, laying her out on the table so I can work the buttons covering her up. She watches me intently, her gaze trained on my face as I slip the buttons through the material, slowly unwrapping her like a Christmas present. Just when her shirt slides apart and my mouth dries at the see-through black lace barely covering her raspberry-colored nipples, looking as sweet as I remember them, my phone rings.

"Shit." I close my eyes and hang my head.

Don't answer it. It's not important.

I grip Abbi's hip. Her eyes narrow as she waits for me to continue or pick up the damn phone.

And I really don't want to answer but what if it's my family? What if they *need* me? The phone stops ringing and I let out a shaky exhale of relief. I'm about to drop my mouth to her taunting breast when the ringing picks up again. I growl out a swear and Abbi's eyebrows dip.

She pops up on her elbows. "Answer it."

"I'm sorry."

"It's fine."

I narrow my eyes at her, trying to read the bend in her eyebrows. *Is it fine?*

I sigh and pull my phone from my pocket. Justine's face lights up the screen. "It's my sister."

Abbi sits up fully and moves to slip past me.

"No." I place my hand on her thigh to keep her ass rooted to the table. "Just do the top few buttons."

"Huh?" she asks.

I swipe right. "Hey, Jus," I answer the FaceTime call.

Instead of Justine, my nieces' adorable smiles light up the screen.

"Uncle Luca!" Laura squeals.

"Uncky! Uncky!" Valentina claps her hands.

"What are you doing?" My nephew Gino appears, his eyes narrowed.

I chuckle and shake my head. "What are you guys doing?"

I look at the time. "It's seven-thirty in the morning. Shouldn't you be at school?"

"It's a PD day," Gino says, looking at me like I'm daft.

"What the hell, er, heck, is that?" I ask.

"Professional development for the teachers," he says like everyone knows that.

"I don't ever remember having those," I tell him.

"That's because you're old," he states matter-of-factly.

My mouth pops open and a soft laugh sounds from Abbi.

"You believe this kid?" I ask her.

"Who are you with?" My other nephew, Jack, appears in the corner of the screen, his expression curious.

"Is it your girlfriend?" Gino, a little shit at ten years old, taunts.

"You have a girlfriend!" Laura claps her hands together. "Can I meet her? Can I?"

I glance at Abbi. "You ready to make this official?"

She rolls her eyes but she's cheesing pretty hard. As much as these little nuggets drive me nuts, I gotta give them props for not making the whole meet-the-family thing a *thing*. Face-Time makes it pretty casual. I wrap my arm around Abbi and pull her to my side, checking that she buttoned up her shirt. When I'm satisfied that no extra skin is showing, I angle the camera and announce, "Guys, this is my girl, Abbi. Isn't she pretty?"

"Sure is," Gino answers automatically.

Abbi laughs, giving a wave. "Hi, guys. I've heard a lot about you."

"You have?" Laura's eyes widen as she looks at Abbi. "You're really beautiful."

"Thank you." Abbi's smile widens. "You're really beautiful, too."

"I pretty too!" Valentina announces, waving her little chubby toddler hand.

"You are a beauty," Abbi agrees.

"What are you all doing with your mom's phone?" I ask Jack.

"Valentina is here since Aunt Nikki had to work. Mom's just in the shower."

"So you thought you'd bug me?" I ask.

Jack shrugs.

"Do you like princesses?" Laura asks Abbi like she's never met a woman before.

"I love princesses," Abbi says. "Mulan is my favorite."

"Mulan? Why?" Laura demands.

"Because she's strong and brave and fights better than all the boys," Abbi explains practically.

Laura nods, thinking this over. "I'm stronger than my brothers."

"Are not." Gino gives her a shove.

I wait for Laura to burst into tears but she just shoots us a wicked grin and twists Gino's nipple through his shirt until he howls.

"This is my family," I explain to Abbi as Justine zips into the room in a towel, her wet hair hanging around her face.

"Jesus Christ! Who did you little fart faces call?" my sister bellows at the kids.

Abbi cracks up as the screen gets jumbled around until my sister's face comes into view.

"Shit," she mutters. "Sorry Luca and—"

"Abbi," Abbi says, lifting her hand to wave again. "It's good to meet you."

My sister's mouth drops open in shock and I take the phone, grinning. "This is my girlfriend, Justine. Turns out I'll be bringing a date to Robbie's dinner next month after all. Gotta go. Love you. 'Bye." I disconnect before my sister can pepper me with questions and interrogate Abbi. She's scarier than Robbie and should be up for promotion at the police station.

The last thing we see before the screen cuts out is Justine's surprised expression.

Abbi laughs again and scoots off the kitchen table. "Your nieces and nephews are cute."

"They're pains in the ass, cock-blocking me before eight in the morning."

Abbi snorts and fiddles with the end of her shirt.

"Now, where were we?" I lift an eyebrow.

But my girl shakes her head. "You promised me breakfast, Luca. Then, I have work."

"No PD day?"

She smacks the back of her hand against my stomach.

I catch it and pull her in for one last kiss. "Pancakes it is," I agree, slipping off the table. "Go get dressed and I'll take you to the best diner on this side of town. You'll be a local in no time."

Abbi blows me a kiss over her shoulder as she walks to her room. I sit in the living room until she appears, making boring black workpants sexy as hell. She slips into winter boots and a coat.

When I reach for her hand, she laces our fingers together.

We step back into the bustling city as a real couple and I like it. I like it a lot.

CHAPTER 11
ABBI

Chloe's face lights up like I announced we're celebrating Christmas twice.

"Seriously? Panda is your boyfriend?" She nearly squeaks.

I roll my eyes, downplaying it because that's what I do. "It's not that big of a deal."

She scoffs. "Not that big of a deal? Abigail Walsh—"

I groan. Only Gran ever called me by my full, antiquated name.

"You haven't referred to a man as your boyfriend since college."

"Don't remind me of Kent," I say, wrinkling my nose.

Chloe's expression mirrors mine. "Don't even think about Kent when we're talking about Panda."

"Right," I agree.

"So"—Chloe waggles her eyebrows—"boyfriend. Damn. I didn't think Panda had it in him."

I laugh lightly. "He's different than I expected."

"In what way?" Chloe leans forward.

"This isn't that juicy."

She shrugs. "Austin is so into hockey that it's pretty much

the only thing we talk about. If I didn't visit Mimi weekly, I'd have nothing interesting in my life to discuss."

I chuckle. Chloe's mimi is a lot like Gran. The reminder makes a strange pang shoot through my chest. Oh, Gran. What would you say if you could see me now? "It's just, Luca's a family man."

Chole's eyebrows shoot up. "A family man?"

I nod. "I met his nieces and nephews on FaceTime this weekend and—"

"You're *meeting* the family?"

"It was FaceTime. Although, his sister did make an appearance in a towel."

"Wait, what?" Chloe laughs.

I back up and tell her the full story, enjoying the expressions that cross her face. When I'm done, she's beaming at me. "Damn, Abs. Luca Pandatelli is, I don't know, heart eyes, for you. He told his sister he was bringing you home? To meet everyone?"

I nod, biting the corner of my mouth to temper my crazy-girl smile. It's impossible and I give in, grinning at my friend. "It's crazy, right? I mean, for six months, nothing, and now, this."

Chloe nods and a bit of the excitement in her eyes dims. "Yes. Just, be careful, Abbi."

"I'm always careful."

"No, you're not." She laughs. "Look, I adore Panda. I think he's funny and charming and he's always reminded me of Drew."

"I miss Drew," I say, referring to Chloe's brother who always looks out for us.

"Me too. But I don't know if Panda's ever been in a real relationship. Like, ever. And you haven't been in one in years—"

"We're not talking about Kent."

"Hell no," she agrees. "Just, make sure you guys are

communicating, okay? I definitely missed the boat on that important relationship builder when things started up with me and Austin."

"I know. This isn't like Kent, who we are not talking about. Or Phil. Luca is…different. Being with him makes me happy."

"Then I'm happy for you." Chloe holds up her coffee mug and I clink mine against it in cheers. "Are things between the sheets still as smoking as summer?"

I blush and wrinkle my nose.

Chloe groans. "Oh, man. Don't tell me that now you're going to clam up. After I've spent the past five years of my life listening to your sexcapades in great detail, now—"

"We haven't slept together again," I admit.

Chloe's mouth drops open. "Seriously?" she sputters.

I nod.

Then, laughter. Not a sweet chuckle or a light laugh. But a bark of loud, uninhibited snorting through the nose laughter. We draw the attention of nearby patrons, even the couple two tables over who are looking at each other with such googly eyes, I'd expect they wouldn't notice a meteor landing in the cafe. But even they narrow their eyes at us in disgust.

"Shh," I tell Chloe.

"Oh my God." She clutches her stomach. "He loves you!"

Jesus. "Chloe." I grip her hand and pull her closer over the table. "Take that back." Just the word *love*, while slightly warming parts of my heart I'm ignoring, could also make me break out in hives.

"Sorry." She clears her throat, trying to school her expression. But her eyes are too damn bright and I roll mine in warning. "It's just, wow. I'm…surprised. All I've heard about Panda since meeting him is that he's always got a flavor of the week. That he wastes no time and is a great—sorry," she cuts herself off.

"No, please continue," I say sarcastically.

She bites back her smile. "The fact that he didn't tap that the second he could"—she points at me—"means he's *really* into you. Like, he might put a ring on it and beg you for little baby Pandas that—"

"All right," I cut her off, glaring at her.

She smirks.

"We're…taking things slow."

"You're in a real relationship." Her tone holds a note of awe that makes me smile.

"I have a boyfriend," I confirm.

Then we both do this weird squee-ing accompanied with jazz fingers. The guy two tables down narrows his eyes further.

"Jeez, with the way he's memorizing his girl's lips, you'd think he'd be happy someone else found love," Chloe mutters and I snort. "So, you're happy?"

"I am."

"Me too. I love that you're in Boston. I love that we're back."

I tap my coffee mug against hers again. "We are most definitely back."

"HONEY, I'M HOME," Luca bellows when he steps into my apartment later that evening.

I quickly blank the screen of my phone where a new, threatening image from Phil appeared an hour ago. Why does he keep sending these to me? What does he want from me?

I toss my phone down and try to forget Phil. The last thing I want to do is ruin things with Luca by talking about Phil and the images he keeps hanging over my head. I close my laptop and look up as he lopes into the living room.

"You should always keep your door locked," he says seriously.

I smile at the protective edge in his tone. "I knew you were coming."

He plops down next to me and takes the laptop from my hands, placing it on the coffee table. "Working?"

"Doing stuff for my gran's estate. How was practice?"

He frowns for a second, his eyes searching mine. "Good," he says finally. "We have a game tomorrow night."

"Tampa."

"Look at you." He grins for real, wrapping an arm around my shoulders and pulling me into his side.

I snuggle closer, rolling the back of my head over his arm. When I meet his gaze, his eyes are dark and serious.

I freeze for one moment, wondering if he knows about Phil's message, which is impossible. But then his gaze drops to my lips, and I lean forward, meeting him for a kiss.

Our lips touch and my body heats, need coursing through me. My hands grip at his hoodie and he repositions me so I'm propped in his lap, straddling him. My palms slide up his chest and over his shoulders, wrapping around the back of his neck.

He lets out a sigh that encourages me to lean forward, to press down on him, to melt into him. His hands palm my ass, one slipping under the fabric of my shirt to glide over my back. I feel his lips curve into a smile when he realizes I'm not wearing a bra. But then his smile hardens and he kisses me with a new ferocity, an intensity that I revel in.

Turning us, Luca lays me down on my couch and hovers over me. He pauses for a moment, pulling his hoodie and shirt clear off his head. I gasp as I take in the lines of his body. Hard chest, abs for days, all muscle and brawn and God—

"You're so fucking sexy," I blurt out.

He smiles, his tongue darting out to swipe across his

bottom lip. "I'm crazy for you, Abbi." His tone is so heartfelt that my breath lodges in my throat.

Luca stares into my eyes and I drown in his and suddenly, every shitty non-relationship I've ever been in makes sense. I was just waiting for *him*. His fingers curl around the waistband of my leggings, his nails tickling me. In one hard tug, he pulls them down to my knees along with my underwear. In the next moment, they're gone completely and I'm sprawled out beneath him in a *The Burnt Clovers* band T-shirt.

Luca wastes no time pushing it up to my collarbone, my breasts spilling out. His eyes widen as he takes me in and he shakes his head. "Christ, you're fucking beautiful. What the hell did I do right to deserve you?" His tone holds a note of awe.

So slowly my breathing ticks up, Luca lowers his head. He licks my nipple like it's a damn ice cream cone before fastening his mouth over my right breast. I arch into him, gasping at the sensation.

Everything about this moment is different than anything I've ever experienced. We're not in the heat of it, drunk and sloppy, in a dark bedroom. Nope. Right now, Luca Pandatelli is studying my body, worshipping it, with the lights on, on a Thursday evening. He's taking his time, testing the weight of my breast on the edge of his fingertips.

He kisses the beauty mark shaped like a strawberry on the side of my ribs. His fingers stroke down my stomach and my knees fall open for him of their own volition.

But he doesn't claim the prize. Not yet.

While I know I should get into this and do something, I'm utterly useless. Instead, I watch Luca's face, commit each emotion that flits over his expression—want, awe, desire, need—to memory. When his fingers drag down my center, I whimper.

"So wet, baby," he murmurs, his eyes holding mine. They're

midnight blue, ringed in slate. He pushes two fingers inside and my eyes close. "Look at me, Abbi," he says, his fingers moving deeper as he settles himself beside me on the couch.

I turn into him, wishing our bodies could just merge in this moment. My hands squeeze his hips before I can slip my hand under his pants, my fingers wrapping around his hard, impressive as fuck length. "No boxers," I comment.

"Was coming home to you," he states. And that word, *home*, does almost as much to my insides as Luca's skilled fingers. His mouth captures mine again and he kisses me like he'll never get enough.

Our movements increase in tempo, our breathing turning into panting as we touch each other like teenagers but with the awareness of adults. Luca's thumb presses against my clit, hard, before softening into a gentle, featherlight touch that keeps me just on the brink.

He manages to tug down his joggers, kicking them off as he repositions over me. His eyes find mine and his Adam's apple bobs, his jawline strained. "Need to grab a condom."

"I'm on the pill."

His eyes widen. "Shit, Abbi. I'm clean."

"Me too."

"You sure about this?"

I nod. I've never been more sure in my life. I always use protection. Double, back-up, can-never-be-safe-enough protection. But with Luca, I *trust* him. It isn't even something I've thought about. It's implicit, a natural extension of all my other feelings.

He positions himself over me and slides inside, moving slowly as my eyes nearly roll back in my head. The sound of my arousal reaches my eardrums and the scent of our combined want scents the air.

Luca swears as he braces his weight over mine, his forearms holding him up as his left hand cups my cheek. He stares straight into my soul as he murmurs, "I'm falling for you, Abbi. Been falling for six goddamn months." Then he slides all the way in and I groan.

He begins to move and I meet his pace, the two of us falling into a rhythm that feels more natural than breathing.

Nothing about our joining is normal for me. Every sensation is heightened, every moment is infused with more. Luca Pandatelli and I make love on my couch on a random evening and my entire world straightens. As I take in his parted lips, steel jawline, and wide eyes brimming with emotions, I know I'll never be the same again. And I don't want to be.

"You're mine, Abbi Walsh. And I take care of what's mine."

His words put me over the edge and I shatter, a thousand insecurities and doubts dissipating in thin air as I come harder than I ever have before. Luca's strangled groan follows close behind and we clutch at each other, steady hands and knowing glances.

When I smile at Luca, it's with the innocence of uncharted territory. I've never felt so certain in my life as I say, "You changed the game for me, Luca."

He drops a sweet kiss to my lips. Then he rolls us sideways, so we're staring at each other, breathing in each other's exhales. "I've fucked up so many things, Abbi. But I swear to you, I won't fuck this up. I'm in love with you, babe."

I press my palm over his heart as I admit, "Me too, Luca. I've been falling for you since the first night we met."

He smiles back, looking more innocent than the hulking hockey god I met in July. "Don't stop, okay? I'll catch you, Abbi. I promise."

I tip my chin up and we kiss, our hands linked together, our hearts finally in sync.

CHAPTER 12
LUCA

I'm on cloud fucking nine.

I whistle as I push into the arena the next day, breathing in the crisp air that's usually stale, lifting my hand to wave to the intern who talks shit behind my back.

Man, today is fucking beautiful.

I enter the locker room, doing a little side shuffle, that garners a hell of a lot of side-eye from a handful of my team-mates. These guys just don't appreciate the little things, the simple joys, the beauty of life.

We're about to skate out onto the ice and play hockey. We're the lucky sons of bitches who turned our childhood dreams into careers. And tonight, my girl is in the stands, rocking my fucking number, cheering *my* name.

I grin. Damn, that feels good.

"What the hell is wrong with you?" Easton asks me, frowning.

"Nothing." I open my locker. "Everything's great."

"Great?" Yaeger narrows his eyes.

I pull off my hoodie and toss it inside, sparing a glance at my friends. "Great," I repeat.

Austin groans and shakes his head.

"What?" James asks him.

Yaeger points at me accusingly. "He met someone."

The guys surrounding me cackle. No damn decency, the lot of them.

"No fucking way," East says.

"I mean, it's believable," Sims pipes up. "Panda meets a lot of someones."

I scratch my cheek with my middle finger and Yeager guffaws.

I close my locker door with a bang and find many sets of eyes trained on me.

I sigh and cross my arms over my chest. "If you must know, Yaeger is correct. I've met someone."

Cheers and jeers sound out and I wait a moment for the locker room to quiet back down.

"Who is she?"

"She gave it to you real fucking good, huh?"

"You seeing her again? Or is she your usual, a one and done?"

The sentences that ring out burn my ears and fill me with shame. Because while I've indulged in locker room talk before, I'm now so disgusted with myself that it takes an extra minute to form coherent thoughts, never mind words.

"Shut the fuck up," I snap and the guys all quiet down, a heaviness settling over the room.

Austin smirks, looking pleased with my outburst while everyone else just looks confused.

"Damn," Yaeger mutters.

"About damn time," Noah adds.

"Gentlemen, I have a girlfriend," I announce.

A few mouths pop open but mostly, my teammates regard me with a mixture of surprise and curiosity.

"And I'm fucking crazy about her," I continue to some applause and cheers. "There will be nothing disrespectful muttered about her. Ever."

Nods and agreeing clucks.

"It's Abbi Walsh," I finish to stunned silence.

"The Outreach Manager?" Yaeger asks.

"She's hot," Sims says matter-of-factly.

I scowl at him.

"Finally." Austin blows out a sigh, clasping me on the back. "Glad you finally pulled your head out of your ass and recognized what was right in front of you."

I nod at Cap.

Noah grins at me. "Good for you, Panda. I like Abbi."

East smirks and shakes his head. "All it took to reform the Hawks notorious player was a fucking good girl."

The guys laugh and I flip them off.

While I've never had an issue with my reputation before, right now, it irks me. I've never been dishonest with women but with Abbi...damn, with Abbi, everything *is* different. By the way the guys are looking at me, they know it too.

I shake off the strange energy and breathe out a sigh of relief when Coach Phillips enters the locker room, clapping his hands and calling us to attention.

Hockey, I can focus on. Relationship chatter, not so much.

It's with gusto that I take the ice, glancing up in the stands to pick out my girl. There she is. I lift a hand in her direction and she beams, her long, dark hair falling over her shoulders as she leans forward.

I grin, she smiles, and the arena seems to shrink. All the fans and players and noise sort of fade out for a second, dim in my head, so I can focus on Abbi.

"Keep your head in the game," James Ryan warns, giving me a knowing glance.

I nod, tearing my eyes away from the most beautiful woman I've ever known. Right now, James is right. I need to focus on the game, on winning.

The New York Sharks line up and I take my position in front of the net. As soon as the whistle blows, the puck drops, and a switch inside my head flips. For as long as I can remember, hockey is the one thing I could do to ensure my family's and my financial stability.

When I hear that whistle, I go all in on preserving that security. Hockey was always my meal ticket—in more ways than one—and even though my feelings are twisted up like crazy, I know better than to take a second of ice time for granted.

After saving every shot on goal during the first period, I miss a snapshot at the start of the second period. My glove grazes the puck and while it's enough to slow its trajectory, it's not enough to block the goal.

Damn. The crowd goes wild as New York ties up with us. I crouch down in front of the net, unwilling to let New York score again. In the third period, Austin scores two goals, giving us a lead that makes breathing a little easier.

I keep my eyes trained on the ice, on the puck. I feel the intensity of every player as their energy rolls off their shoulders and crashes down on me. But true to my word, I save every shot that comes at me, and we win 3-1.

My heart races as the final whistle sounds out. Tonight was different. I was nervous, not because thousands of people were watching, cursing me out for my missed block, or commenting on the team. But because for the first time, there was a woman in the stands, watching *me*. Abbi is *my woman* and it made all the difference.

"Your girl's got hearts in her eyes," Yaeger comments as we make our way back to the locker room.

I snort and smack him on the back.

"I'm serious, she never dragged her eyes away from you. But man does she know the game."

"Huh?"

"Every time I looked up, she was on her feet, shouting out commands. She knows her shit. You picked a good one,

Panda." He bumps his shoulder against mine before cutting to his locker.

I tilt my head, recalling something she said the first night she met me. *I like the players, hate the game.*

At the time, I thought she meant she didn't like hockey. I thought she wasn't into sports, just players. I open my locker door and consider Yaeger's words. Maybe she enjoyed tonight more than I thought she would?

The thought makes me grin because hell, a girl who shows up in my number, follows the game, *and* enjoys it? That's some relationship hat trick shit right there.

I shower quickly, answer a few post-game questions, and head out. While I usually hang around, kick it with some of the reporters, or try to wrangle the guys into after-game drinks, tonight, I just want to see Abbi.

I turn the corner and she appears before me, leaning up against a wall, sandwiched between Chloe and Claire.

Her face lights up when she sees me and I find myself cheesing back until my cheeks hurt.

"Aww," Claire coos.

I ignore her though. I only have eyes for Abbi and when she pushes off the wall and bounds toward me, I'm ready to catch her and wrap her up tight.

She laughs as I lift her, her legs encircling my hips. "You were amazing," she gushes, fueling my ego, which the guys would argue doesn't need any help.

"Did you have fun?" I ask her, moving toward the parking lot.

"Panda, wait. Aren't we getting drinks?" Sims calls out.

"Don't you want to play some video games?" Yaeger tacks on.

"Come chill with your team," Austin bellows.

I hear the laughter float behind me. I raise a hand and flip them all the middle finger again, their laughter growing raucous. Abbi chuckles in my ear before kissing a trail up the side of my neck, her teeth nipping my earlobe.

We walk out of the arena amid cheers and whistles and I love that my girl isn't embarrassed in the slightest. If anything, she encourages it, surprising even me.

"You sure aren't shy," I tell her, kissing her hard before letting her slide down my body and settling her on her feet.

"Can't say that I am," she agrees, slipping an arm around my waist.

I lead us toward my SUV, liking the way she fits beside me. "I've never had this before," I tell her truthfully as I open the passenger door.

Her forehead wrinkles as she looks up at me. "Had what?"

"This." I gesture between us. "I never had a real girlfriend before. Not one to rock my number and watch my games and have it…mean something. Thank you for cheering us on tonight."

Her expression softens and she reaches up to brush my hair back. Gripping the side of my head she says, "I don't know what to do with you, Luca. You've got a tough shell but you say the sweetest things."

I laugh, dipping my head.

"Are you blushing?" Her tone holds a note of amusement.

"No." I laugh, palming her face.

She snorts into my hand. "I like that I can make you blush," she admits and I drop my hand in time to read the seriousness in her expression.

"The night we met, you said you like the players, just not the game…" I trail off.

Recognition flares in her eyes and she groans. "I was an idiot. I was just…hurt about…stuff."

"Phil," I state.

She shrugs and slips inside the SUV. For a second, I think

she's going to shut me out but then she angles her body outwards, her feet resting on the running board.

"What happened, Abbi?"

She licks her lips and looks me in the eye. "We're really doing this, huh?"

"Doing what?"

"Having this conversation."

"I'd like to," I say truthfully. "I want to know everything about you, Abbi. Everything you're willing to share."

She sighs, her eyes tender. "I don't know what to do with you, Luca. You're unlike any man I've ever met and—"

"I've heard this before," I joke, swiveling my hips.

She snorts, shooting me a grateful look for the levity I'm apt to provide. "It scares me," she admits on a whisper.

"Baby." I lean even closer, my hand sliding off the top of the car to cup her cheek. "You don't have to be scared. I just want to…know you, Abbi. Really know you. With no secrets and head games and bullshit."

She nods slowly, biting the corner of her mouth. "I'd like that. It's just…*this* is hard."

"I get that," I say, knowing exactly how she feels. Just a few weeks ago, I told her how much she scares me. "I don't just let anyone meet my nieces and nephews."

She laughs.

"No." I touch her knee. "I'm serious. I know how I come off to people, fun-loving, outgoing, crazy Panda. But my family is my life, Abbi. And for most people, they don't exist because I don't share them."

Her eyes widen as she realizes what I'm really telling her. *I trust you. I want you in my life.*

She takes the hand that's holding her knee and laces our fingers together. Bringing our joined hands to her mouth, she kisses my knuckles.

"Phil was a football player," she starts.

I swear, already disliking him. Abbi narrows her eyes.

I widen mine back. "Football? Really?"

She chuckles before her expression falls. "We worked together on outreach programs."

I nod, remembering how Austin said Abbi did youth football outreach for the Kings. "So, you like athletes," I surmise.

"Sometimes," she shoots back, her voice sad. "I thought he was divorced."

I close my eyes and sigh, knowing where she's going with this. I've seen it happen a million times. Professional athlete with adoring fans, especially sexy, tempting female fans, who profess living one life while actually living another. You know, the one with a wife and kids at home that are conveniently overlooked.

"I remember when his marriage went south; it was all over the tabloids," she adds defensively.

I nod, working a swallow. A sense of foreboding builds in my chest as a metallic taste fills my mouth.

"They were in marriage counseling. Not divorced at all," she sighs. "Because he was well-known, divorce was being speculated. I mean, TMZ was all over it. His wife, Melanie, didn't want to give the tabloids any information to use against them, so she begged him to just let things play out publicly while the two of them worked on their relationship privately. But at the time, I didn't know any of that. He said yes to her so he could feed bullshit lies to me about how his marriage was already over, and divorce proceedings were underway." Tears fills her eyes, and she blinks furiously. "Can you imagine how I felt when a few months pass and she's pregnant? They're on the front of *People* magazine with her hand on her adorable baby bump and him cradling her in his arms?" Her voice breaks and she clears her throat. "The whole thing was just awful, especially because Phil is the first man I really saw a future with after my college boyfriend, Kent, cheated on me with my sorority sister. He got her pregnant," she snorts, tossing her hands in the air. "Apparently, that's a theme in my life."

"Shit," I mutter, rubbing at my forehead with my free hand. "I'm sorry, baby. I can't imagine dealing with all that... turmoil."

She shakes her head. "That's not the worst part."

"What's the worst part?" I ask, a thread of fear skating over my spine.

She pauses, blowing out a deep breath. Then she steels her shoulders, meets my gaze, and says, "There are photos. Of us. Me. That's why Phil called me that night when I was at your place. He's been...threatening to leak them."

CHAPTER 13
ABBI

"Pictures," he repeats, looking confused.

Shit. I mentally berate myself for being so honest. I shouldn't have told Luca about the photos with Phil.

What if he wants to *see* them? A sick sense of dread sweeps through me at the possibility. The poses, burned into my retina, flare to life in my mind. I'm dressed sexy as hell, in the most provocative positions I've ever ventured into. I'm a little bit drunk, a lot breathless, and thirsty as fuck. It shows in the images, adding to my mortification.

Will Luca be disgusted? Or worse, will he see them and *know* how pathetic I am? How needy I was, how much I prayed that someday, a man would want me back?

I chew the corner of my mouth, waiting for him to connect the dots. I'm staring right at his face so I can witness, up close and personal, as his confusion gives way to understanding which morphs into fury.

"What kind of fucking pictures?" he snaps.

I roll my lips together and widen my eyes, hoping my non-verbal answer will suffice.

"Fuck." He grips the back of his neck, turning his face away for a moment.

My insides twist, knotting together until nausea rolls through my stomach.

"What a fucking piece of shit." Luca's face snaps back toward mine. "How could he do that to you? What's his last name? Phil what?"

My mouth pops open and I stare at him.

"Tell me," he demands, the veins in his forearm popping as he leans even lower.

"You're not mad?" I ask.

He frowns. "Of course, I'm mad. I'm fucking furious that some guy would expose you like that. Put you in this position. Take something personal, private and—what?"

I sputter. "I mean, you're not mad at *me*?"

Understanding followed by compassion douses his expression as he shakes his head. He drops my hand and pulls me into a hug. He's half in, half out of the car and I think about how ridiculous we must look to anyone passing by.

But Luca keeps his arms wrapped around me and the longer he holds me, the more I relax into his embrace. That he cares about *me* more than the possibility that the pictures may leak and circulate among his team, is very telling of the kind of man he is. Tears rush forward as I breathe him in, hope swelling in my chest.

I was prepared for his anger. For an outburst of hurtful words and his rejection. Instead, Luca shows me understanding, empathy, and love. And it guts me.

"I could never be mad at you, Abbi," he says soothingly. His words wash over me like a salve, dulling past hurts and making my skin tingle.

I bury my face into the crook of his neck and breathe him in. His body is warm, even after standing in the cold, and I press myself against him, more than comforted by his presence. Right now, I need him and he's here for me in a way that no man has been before.

He blows out a sigh and pulls away, giving me a searching look. "Is he why you lost your job?"

I nod, my chin quivering.

Luca swears again and grips my chin. His thumb draws a line down the center of my chin before swiping along my jaw. He shakes his head, his voice lower, rougher. "You still haven't told me his last name."

"Rickens."

He blanches. "Phil Rickens?"

"Heard of him?"

"He's a fucking tool. I met him once and…damn, Abbi."

I shrug, averting my gaze, even though my throat tightens.

"No." Luca lifts my face again. "Don't pull away from me. If we're really going to do this"—he signals between us—"then we can't hide from each other. I don't know a lot about relationships, Abbi, but I've been on the periphery of enough to know that this, the beginning, is the easiest. Things will only get harder from here on out."

A chuckle drops from my mouth, surprising us both. I tip my head back farther. "Well, that's a relief to hear."

Luca smiles, running the pad of his thumb down the center of my chin again before releasing it. "Nothing we can't handle, baby."

"I want your confidence."

"You've got confidence in spades."

"Then, I want your certainty. Your belief in…the future."

The corners of his eyes crinkle as he smiles at me. "Future's all hopeful, babe."

I nod slowly, plucking his words out of the air like wishes and tucking them safely away for future study.

He dips his head and kisses me, his tongue slipping into my mouth. His kiss is more insistent than safe, probing instead of pacifying. "Let me take you home now, Abbi."

"You don't want to hang with the team?" I pull back, surprised.

"I want to hang with my girl."

"We can swing by Taps first."

"No way," Luca growls. "I need to get you home and erase any fucking memory of Phil fucking Rickens."

I toss my head back and laugh as Luca grins at me. "I'm serious," he says.

"Take me home then, Luca."

He leans into the car again to pull my seat belt across my chest. Then, he closes the door and jogs around to the driver's side, sliding inside and turning on the ignition.

He looks over at me, all bedroom eyes and a strong jaw. "He won't hurt you again. No one will."

I offer him a soft smile, even though I know better than to believe such promises. Still, his words fill me with longing. A yearning that beats in my chest and extends behind my ribs, dropping lower until I squeeze my thighs together. The resolve in Luca's tone is too strong, too honest, to oppose. And right now, I don't want to think about reality. I just want to be here with him. In this moment.

I reach over the center console and wrap my hand around his forearm. "Take me home now, Luca."

He puts the car in drive.

LUCA'S EYES blaze as he settles over me. My breath hitches as I stare into his eyes, two bottomless pools of blue.

Little warning bells clang in my head. This is still new. Remember what happened over the summer?

But my guard has already come down. How could it not?

Luca's hand sweeps up my side, feathering over the

Hawks logo on the front of my jersey. I'm stretched out in the center of his bed, my jeans already in a pile on the floor.

He lost his shirt the second we crossed the threshold into his room and his jeans, worn and ripped, hang low on his hips, the button already popped for easy access.

"Love seeing you in my number, Abs," he mutters, dropping his head. His lips find the side of my neck as his hand snakes underneath my jersey until he palms my breast.

I turn my head, our noses grazing. For one long beat, our eyes hold. Then I tip my chin and he drops his face and our lips meet, molding together in an instant. I roll onto my side, Luca's fingers brushing over my bra-covered nipple. He touches me slowly, exploring my skin, while his mouth spills desires into mine.

He pulls back, rolling the jersey up and over my head, leaving it splayed against the pillows at the head of his bed. His gaze scans my body, his breathing kicks up a notch as the tip of his tongue slips through his lips. One of his hands locks around both of my wrists, keeping my arms up over my head.

Rocking a black lace bra and matching thong, I love how Luca's eyes flare with heat. His eyes drink me in like they'll never get their fill and I revel under his attention.

"You're so sexy, Abbi," he breathes out, swallowing thickly. His eyes hold mine. "So fucking sexy," he repeats, dropping his mouth again.

I shift beneath him, helping him settle in between my thighs as I arch into his touch. He keeps kissing me as he expertly removes his jeans and I giggle into his mouth.

When he pauses to meet my eyes, I jut my chin down his frame.

"Done this before, huh?" I wrinkle my nose.

He grins and shakes his head. "It's never meant this much."

Swoon. I die. How the hell does this man manage to undo me with *words*?

But his words make my heart race and my mind quiet and my body quiver with need for…more of him.

I wrap my arms around his back, loving how the muscles in his shoulders roll under my touch. I hitch myself closer to him, deepening our kiss until he moans. My hands track the planes of his back, lower until I can slip my fingers under the waistband of his boxer briefs and help him work those off.

He springs free, hard against my upper thigh, and heat floods me. I crave Luca Pandatelli in a way I never desired a man before. It's because of his words, his heart, him.

I kiss him harder as he flicks open my bra and tugs my thong to the side. His fingers sweep over my core, and he groans again.

"Jesus, you're perfect. So fucking wet," he says, his voice guttural.

I watch as he sucks off my sweetness, my eyes nearly rolling back in my head.

"Look at me," he commands and I force my eyes open. "Watch."

I do as he says, my breathing turning ragged as he drags the head of his cock through my folds. My desire glistens off of him and I couldn't tear my eyes away if I tried.

I watch with rapt attention as he enters me, moving at a deliciously slow pace that I feel throughout my body like a livewire.

"Fuck," he moans.

"Don't stop," I say, clenching around him.

His hand settles at the base of my throat, his thumb swiping over my clavicle. "Never."

He kisses me hard and my eyes close. I sink into the sensations coursing through my body, losing myself to this moment, this man.

"More," I murmur.

He increases the pace, his mouth moving over mine with urgency, his body pressing into mine with an edge. We come together hard and fast, both of us shattering at the same moment.

But instead of turning away, Luca continues to kiss me. His tongue laps against mine, his urgency slows into a sweetness. His touch is featherlight as it rolls over my skin.

I keep my legs wrapped around his lower back, erasing any space between us.

We barely have time to recover from round one before round two heats up. This time, it's slow and languid. This time he makes love to me, savoring my sounds and swallowing my kisses.

"I'm all in with you, Abbi," he murmurs, dragging his tongue down the shell of my ear.

I gasp as he enters me again, so slowly my thighs tremble for the sweetest release that only he can provide.

"Luca, please."

"Please what, sweet baby?" he teases, peppering my throat with kisses.

"Need you."

He slides in all the way and I grip his shoulders.

"Want you," he replies.

"I'm yours, Luca," I tell him the truth.

A ghost of a smile flickers over his lips as he gazes down at me. Then, he rolls us until I'm straddling his hips and he's looking up at me, his eyes hooded. "Show me."

I smile, lifting up an inch at a time before plunging back down on him.

He swears, his hands gripping my hips.

"You're going to kill me, Abbi."

I smirk, brace my palms on his chest, and lean forward to kiss him hard. "I'm going to make you come undone," I promise him.

He groans but his eyes heat. "Do it," he nearly begs.

So, I do. Twice.

CHAPTER 14
LUCA

"The promotion dinner is in three weeks," Nikki says on FaceTime.

"I'll be there," I promise.

"I know." She rolls her eyes. "What I want to know is if you're bringing your *girlfriend*."

I snort. "You don't have to say it like that. I'm not in high school. This isn't some random, short-lived experience."

Nikki beams. "You really care about this woman, huh?"

"I do."

"She's very pretty."

At this, I narrow my eyes. "Where'd you see her picture?"

"Seriously?" My sister gives me a look.

For an instant, Abbi's confession about Phil and the photos blares in my mind and I feel like I might be sick.

"You guys are trending on Insta. Hashtag Hockey's Cutest Couple. You guys populate the feed."

I let out a laugh. "Damn. Well, you're right, Abbi is gorgeous."

"I can't wait to meet her."

"Three weeks," I confirm. "We'll fly in early. I want her to meet Pop and all of you ahead of time, so she's not over-whelmed."

"Aww." Nikki smirks.

"Don't say it all sweetly. You know our family is crazy and has no respect for personal boundaries."

"One-hundred percent. I guess I should be happy Larry lasted as long as he did. Although it would have been better if he split before we exchanged vows."

A rush of anger crashes over me and I swear.

Nikki clucks her tongue. "Too soon?" I glare at her and she shrugs. "Humor is how I cope."

"How's Valentina? Is her new inhaler doing the job?"

"Yes, thank you," my sister sighs. Then she fills me in about my niece, the appointment she has with a specialist next month, and shares bits of gossip about my brothers and Justine.

When I hang up with Nikki, I check the time. Abbi should be here with takeout any second and after a grueling week, I can't wait to spend time with my girl.

Although she crawls into my bed every night and I wake up and kiss her each morning, we've both been living full days without much time to connect.

I know it's only been a short time, barely a month, but I miss her. And I want to see her. Three days ago, I left a key for her on the nightstand. I had already left for my run by the time she woke up but she sent me a picture of the Hawks keychain she attached it to.

When I hear the key turn in the lock, I sit straight up on the couch, turning toward the front door. It swings open and Abbi walks inside, immediately brightening the atmosphere and improving my mood.

I hop over the back of the couch to help her with the takeout bags. "What'd you get?"

"Mexican."

"Yes!" I cheer, peeking inside and grinning when I spot

the logo for the fusion place Noah got me into. "I love their sushi fajitas."

Abbi wrinkles her nose at the combo. "That's good, because that's what I got you."

I kiss her cheek. "Best girlfriend ever."

She swats my ass and moves to the kitchen to grab some plates and utensils. We sit at my kitchen island and dig into our dinners. I look at her, noting how normal this is. No awkwardness, no ulterior motives. Just me and my girl having a meal on a Thursday night. I smile and pop the tab on a sparkling water.

"What?" Abbi asks when she finds me staring at her. She flashes me a grin. "Do I have spinach in my teeth?"

"No, goof." I pinch her cheek. "I was just thinking how nice this is."

"Nice?" She lifts an eyebrow.

I nod, taking a swig of my water. "It's just so...normal. Comfortable. I never got what the hell my friends were talking about when they said they were just kicking it with their girl. I used to wonder what the hell they did after they came."

She snorts.

"But now I know"—I gesture between us—"and I like it."

She grins. "I'm glad. Because I like hanging with you too."

"Tell me about your day," I say, taking a bite of my fajita.

Abbi chuckles but indulges me. "You're right, we're really nailing this relationship thing."

"Right," I agree, gesturing for her to continue.

"Okay, so, I'm thinking about a potential hockey camp for spring break."

"Hockey camp?"

"Yes. All of the public and Catholic schools are closed the same week. What if two or three players each take an afternoon, or a morning session, and run some meet-and-greets, complete with drills? We can break it up by age group and introduce hockey to the new kids and run something a little more competitive for the kids who already play. But I bet there would be a lot of interest since parents still have to work that week. We could charge a small fee, or maybe make it free? I don't know, I need to run the logistics past Mark, but I think that would be a good week to do something big."

I nod, turning over the idea. "The timing could work. I mean, it's still regular season."

"Right? And it wouldn't be a full day commitment. We'd rotate players, coaches, staff." She pops a chip with salsa into her mouth. "Just an idea."

"It's a good one."

"Thank you. How was your day?"

I prattle on about a stupid stunt Yaeger pulled with an ice bath and Abbi laughs, rolling her eyes at our antics. We settle into the conversation, chatting about random things, before relocating to the couch to watch the new Spider-Man movie.

With my arm wrapped around Abbi, I wonder how the hell I missed out on this for so long. My friends were right. Hanging with my girlfriend is awesome. For the first time in my life, I'd rather be exactly where I am instead of on the ice, or drinking beers with the guys on my team, or playing video games.

"What?" Abbi hisses, turning toward me.

I stare back at her, grinning.

She raises her eyebrows, waiting.

"I love you, Abbi Walsh. That's all."

She stares at me for a long moment before a smile spreads across her face. "You do?" she asks softly.

"I do," I say simply, owning the truth. Because when you love someone, you should tell them.

"I love you too, Luca."

I grin and kiss her temple. "I like watching movies with you."

She chuckles. "I like doing everything with you."

"Noted," I say, flipping off the movie.

"What?" She screeches as I lift her over my shoulder. "What are you doing? Put me down?" She laughs. "I thought we were talking."

"You said everything," I explain, moving toward my bedroom.

"So?"

"So, why the hell would we watch a movie when you'll enjoy this even more?" I toss her in the center of my bed.

She laughs loudly as she bounces up and down.

I smirk, reaching behind my head to pull off my shirt.

Abbi's laughter fades as she drinks in my body, her cheeks heating. She's still smiling when she meets my gaze but her eyes are serious. "I've never met anyone like you, Luca."

"That's a good thing." I drop to the bed and move over her as she lies back. "Because I've never felt like this about anyone before." Then, I kiss her and show her just how fucking good she makes me feel.

FEBRUARY ROLLS into March as I settle into my new normal.

Hockey still rules my life but now, my days pass quicker. I'm eager to hit my workouts hard, doing the most effective training in the least amount of time. I like coming home after a game instead of swinging by Taps so I can catch Abbi before she falls asleep. Basically, I just want to spend as much time with my girl as possible.

Our schedules—with my hockey commitments and her planning a spring break camp—are hectic. Two weeks after I told Abbi I love her, I'm traveling back from Atlanta after a tough game.

We lost in overtime and morale on the plane is low. I'm exhausted, stressed about my shitty performance on the ice, and desperately wanting to slide into bed beside Abbi and sink into her, letting her chase my frustration away like only she can.

"What's up, Nikki?" I answer my sister's call on the Bluetooth as I pull out of the arena.

"Sorry about Atlanta."

"Yeah," I mutter, not in the mood to rehash the game.

"Just wanted to check that you're still flying in on Friday?"

"Yep. Friday night, Abbi and I will be there." I take a left turn. "I want to spend some time with Pop too so we're spending the weekend."

"Yay! We can't wait to meet her," Nikki says.

"You're gonna love her." Some of the heaviness in my chest eases as I pull in front of my building.

"You know this is the first girl you've ever brought home."

"I know." I drive around back to the parking garage. "Listen, Nik, I'm just getting home and—"

"Don't finish that sentence," Nicole laughs. "I just wanted to remind you to send me your flight details. We'll have dinner at Justine's Friday night. Just pizza and pasta, casual."

"Sounds good." I grin, knowing my family's definition of casual is still excessive. I hope Abbi isn't overwhelmed but the truth is, everything my family does, is done on a grand, loud, boisterous scale. "See you Friday."

"Night, Luca."

I end the call and drive down into the parking garage. I pull into my spot and let out a slow exhale. Now that I'm home, I feel lighter than I have for the past two days. How the hell do the guys on my team leave their wives, their kids, all season long for games?

I used to question the guys who would rather go back to

their hotel rooms and FaceTime their preschoolers instead of hitting a club but now, I kind of get it. I also kind of want it.

The consistency, the certainty, the missing. Because I've sure as hell missed Abbi the past two days and text messages and a FaceTime barely made the distance manageable.

I grab my coat and head toward the elevator. When I enter my condo, the lights are off except for the undermount kitchen lighting. It casts the space in a pale glow, downtown Boston and bits of the Harbor stretching for as far as I can see out of the floor-to-ceiling windows.

I drop my coat on a barstool and quietly stand in the doorframe of my bedroom.

There she is. Dark hair curling over my pillow, sweeping eyelashes, and a pouty mouth—Abbi Walsh looks like an angel. My angel. I shed my clothes and plug in my phone. Dropping to the bed, I hover over her, brushing her hair back from her face. I grin as she flinches in her sleep, loving the expressions she makes.

She stirs, her body turning toward mine, like a gravitational pull. "Luca?"

"I'm here, baby," I whisper, kissing her cheek. "Shh, sleep."

She doesn't respond but her lips twitch the slightest bit, a soft smile on her gorgeous face. I pull her into my arms and hold her, resting my chin on top of her hair. Her slight snores hum in the air, her breath tickling my chest.

I like seeing her like this, all innocent and trusting. I love that she's let her guard down with me, that I can confide in her. That we're building something I never thought I'd find. Because God, it's the best with her.

"Good night, baby." I kiss the crown of her head, settling back against the pillows with her in my arms.

As I drift to sleep, I think about what a lucky bastard I am. How did I ever deserve a woman like Abbi?

CHAPTER 15
ABBI

It happens on a Wednesday. In an instant, everything changes.

It's a subtle shift in the air, an extra-long glance, a whisper behind folded fingers.

And I know.

Dread settles in the pit of my stomach, expanding outward until I feel both sick and numb. My fingers tremble, the rolled-up poster board in my hand rustling.

A sympathetic cluck. A judgey side-eye. An aversion of eye contact.

Tears prick the corners of my eyes as I pick up my pace, slipping into my office and closing the door. I drop the posters on the edge of my desk. My shoulder bag, heavy with two binders for all of the March break camp preparation, lands on the floor with a thud.

I pull my phone out and wince at the flood of messages lighting up my screen. It's out in the open now, everyone knows.

Shame clogs my throat and my mind races.

Will I lose my job? Will Luca leave me? Will Boston turn

into Hoboken part two, and I'll be forced to start over again? Will this follow me for the rest of my life?

PHIL

I told you not to get too comfortable.

He sent the message along with an image of me and Luca, walking down Boyleston Street hand in hand. I blanche, my anger rising in red hot waves. Phil leaked the photos because I moved on? Wasn't destroying my career in NJ enough?

A disturbing thought rolls through my mind and I wince. *Thank God Gran isn't here to witness this.*

My gran, with her kind eyes, strong hugs, and bold cocktail rings, would be mortified to know that the girl she raised turned into a woman who could star in a porno. That there are pictures out there, on the Internet for everyone and anyone to see, and that they will live on forever.

My phone screen lights up every three seconds with new messages, with awful Tweets and social media comments, with missed calls. I'm relieved it's on silent and I turn it facedown on my desk, dropping my face into my hands.

You're okay. You're going to get through this. Everything is—

The door to my office swings open and I jump, my mouth dropping open when I see Chloe.

"How bad?" I ask her.

She swears and closes the door behind her. She rounds my desk and pulls me into her arms, hugging me tightly. "Indy sent it to me."

"Indy?" I ask, wondering how the hell Indy stumbled across my photos.

"The students in one of her classes…"

I wince, squeezing my eyes closed. Of course. If someone suddenly becomes a social media meme or trending Insta hashtag, the college crowd pounces. God, what must she think of me?

"What did Panda say?" Chloe asks, pulling back to sit in the chair across from my desk.

"Nothing yet. I just, you're the first person I…" I take a deep breath. "I haven't looked at all the messages on my phone yet."

"Good," Chloe declares, swiping my phone up. She drops it into her purse without glancing at the screen and for that, I'm grateful.

"Thanks for coming."

She rolls her eyes. "Stop. I'm always here for you."

"Good. Because I need you to break me out of here and take me to the nearest bar."

Chloe pauses, studying me. Her eyes, a bright green, gleam like a cat's as she sees all the things I want to hide. But she's been my best friend since high school and knows me better than…well, anyone now that Gran passed. "Do you want to call Panda?"

Horror washes over me at the realization that I'm going to have to talk about *this* with Luca. "God no," I blurt out, feeling nauseous. "I want to pretend that this isn't happening. That I'm not reliving the past eight months of my life. That my job isn't in jeopardy and I didn't just fuck shit up with the man I lo—" I clamp my mouth shut.

Chloe's eyes widen. "You love him?"

"Shit."

Her expression softens. "I'm so sorry you're dealing with this, Abs. But maybe you should talk to him? Explain everything? It will be better coming from you than someone else."

"I'm sure he already knows. And he hasn't reached out to me." I point to my office phone, not knowing if Luca tried to call my cell. Even if he did, he's one of the few people who could get in touch with me if he really wanted to.

As if on cue, my office phone rings and I jump again, my nerves already shredded.

Chloe looks at me for a long moment before reaching across my desk and picking it up.

"Hello? Sorry, she's unavailable at the moment. May I take a message?"

I slide a pen and pad of yellow Post-its closer to Chloe and she jots down a name and number.

"Sounds great, thanks. Okay, bye." She hangs up the phone and glances at me nervously.

"What now?" I ask, knowing that more bad news can only follow something like this. How bad will the fallout be? How destructive will my reaction be?

"That was Mr. Miller from Melrose Middle School."

"They're pulling out of the camp, aren't they? Shit, I didn't even think that this whole project could fall apart because of, because I—"

"Phil's a fucking douchebag," Chloe interjects.

Her outrage pacifies me the tiniest amount and I cling to that small win. At least my best friend is still standing by my side. At least I can rely on Chloe.

"And I don't know what he wants. He just asked you to call him," she offers, not sounding hopeful at all.

I shrug and blow out a deep breath. "Margaritas?"

"Abbi," Chloe says slowly, "you can't just drink your way through this."

"Want a bet?"

"Talk to Panda."

I shake my head. "I can't. I mean, he knows about the photos but—"

"He does?"

I nod. "I told him. But knowing something exists and seeing it"—I shake my head—"two completely different things. I can't, I'm not ready to talk to him about this. Please, Chlo," I plead with her.

"All right," she agrees, picking up my shoulder bag. "Jesus, this is heavy. You need anything else?"

I shake my head, knowing she has my phone.

"Put on your coat. I'll venture out first and let you know when it's safe to follow." Chloe moves to the door.

I snort, knowing how ridiculous this is. I'm a grown woman, thirty-one years old, independent, smart, and motivated. What I do on my own time, in my personal life, should be private. If I was a man, I'd be getting calls of congratulations and having strangers slap me on the back.

But because I'm a woman, I'm about to be slut-shamed in every facet of my life. I can feel the dark cloud hovering just out of reach but soon, it will be pouring on my head and when it does, I want to be drunk. Or at least a little tipsy. Just enough to handle things with humor instead of rage.

I zip my coat and flip up the hood, waiting by the door for Chloe's signal.

"Coo, co-coo," she lets out a fucking bird call that makes me laugh despite the fact that my life is spinning out of control.

I follow her out of my office, down a stairwell, and out into the cold air and winter sunshine. We make a run for it, the two of us laughing even though nothing is funny.

When I slide into the passenger seat of her car, my laughs turn into sobs and then, tears. Big, fat tears that roll down my cheeks. I drop my head into my hands and ugly cry like a woman who just discovered naked photos of her are making their rounds at her work, among her friends, all over the damn city.

Oh wait, that's me.

"You're going to be okay, Abbi. I promise." Chloe reaches over and pulls me into a hug.

I'm sure I will. But what about Luca? How will he live this down? Will he even want me after this? "What if he doesn't forgive me?"

"Panda?" Chloe pulls back.

I nod, scrubbing my fingers across my eyes. The tips come

away black with mascara and I moan, knowing I must look like a drowned raccoon.

Chloe reaches into her center console and removes a packet of makeup cleansing wipes.

I give her a look and she shrugs, plucking one out and passing it to me.

"Panda's gonna step up for you. He's probably got a hundred dick pics circulating right along with—" I cut her a look and she stops talking. "Sorry, that was insensitive. I was just trying to lighten the mood."

"Don't try so hard," I advise. "Just…take me to the tequila."

Chloe pulls her seat belt across her chest and flips the ignition. "Jolene's here we come."

I lean back in my seat, staring out the window as the Boston city streets blur past. It's too bad I was really starting to like it here. Where will I move to next?

I rub my fingers over my temples, trying to reframe my thoughts. I search for a sliver of positivity, for something good that I can pluck out of this scenario and focus on.

But the thought that persists is an image of Luca. Disappointment in his eyes, disgust in the twist of his mouth, and hurt in the lines of his face. He'll never forgive me for splashing him all over social media as the hockey player who fell for a whore.

Bitterness explodes in my mouth at the word. I hate derogatory words used against women like weapons but right now, I can't conjure up a different description.

CHAPTER 16
LUCA

I feel it the second I step into the locker room. The way the joking around immediately stops, the awkwardness that hangs over the space like a joke gone wrong, the pity in my teammates' eyes and faces as they both stare at me and avert their gazes.

"What's going on?" I ask, nervousness zipping through me. I stopped by the trainers after practice but something definitely happened in the past fifteen minutes.

By the worried looks on my teammates' faces and lack of conversation, it's obvious that the something has to do with me. My unease flares to life as my thoughts take a nosedive.

Is Valentina in the hospital? Did Pop have another heart attack? Is Ricky deploying? How did my team learn about it before me?

I look around the space for Coach Phillips or someone from HR but it's just the guys.

"What the hell happened?" I snap, my hands curling into fists. Adrenaline eats some of my fear, putting me on edge. Whoever it is, I can handle it is. Whatever it is, I'll deal with it.

"It's Abbi," Austin says slowly.

Except that. The blood drains from my face and a fear I've never known spreads through my body, infects my bloodstream, cuts me off at the goddamn knees.

Abbi. My Abbi.

My chest aches and I press against it, as if checking that I've still got a heartbeat.

"What happened?" I murmur, my thoughts spiraling.

Is she sick? Was she in an accident? Is she in the hospital, needing me?

My gaze darts around the room, mentally willing one of the guys on the team to tell me what the fuck is going on so I can...do something. Something other than stand here in the worst goddamn limbo I've ever been in.

"Panda." Easton shuffles forward, his eyes solemn. And fuck, if East is being serious, then it's really bad.

"Is she okay?" I close my eyes.

"Yes," Easton replies and my eyes fly open. "Physically, she's fine."

Physically? I frown, my eyebrows snapping together as I try to make sense of what he's *not* saying.

Austin passes me his phone and I take it, suddenly scared to look at the screen. I know the moment I do, everything will be different. Changed.

Just this morning, I fixed Abbi a cup of coffee, left it on the end table, and kissed her temple goodbye before my morning run. I thought about how things in my life were finally looking up, how things were starting to click and make sense, how I could *see* my future.

I chuckle, the sound jarring in the somber atmosphere. Clearly, that was a mistake. Whatever is on Austin's phone is going to change everything and I'm not sure I want to see it.

"All right, let's give Panda a minute," Noah says, clapping his hands together.

The guys all look away and throw themselves back into the task of getting dressed, pulling hoodies over their heads, tying the laces of their sneakers. They slam their locker doors and shoulder practice bags.

Not one of them looks at me as they shuffle out of the locker room. Austin holds the door open, exchanging words with the team that I don't catch.

My heartbeat is too loud in my temples. Saliva floods my mouth, pooling as even swallowing seems difficult. What the hell is going on?

"You're going to be okay," Noah offers, smacking me on the back. "You want me to stick around?"

I shake my head. "No, no, I'm fine."

"Let us know if you need anything," Easton says, following his brother out of the locker room.

Silence descends. The only sound is a dripping faucet from the shower area and Cap's and my breathing.

"How bad is it?" I ask my captain.

Austin leans against the closed locker room door, folding his arms over his chest. "It depends."

"On?"

"How deep are you in with Abbi?"

Fuck. I glare at him, not sure if I want to swing at him or hug him. "I love her," I say, no hesitation.

His eyes widen and he straightens against the door.

"Weren't expecting that?" I ask, my tone harsh.

He shakes his head, rolling his lips together. "No. And I'm not sure if that makes it better or worse. Look, what's on that—"

"Is she stepping out on me?" I ask, a thought I never considered popping out of my mouth. I wince, hating that I'm even doubting Abbi. But what other explanation fits these circumstances?

"No," Austin's voice doesn't waver and I breathe out a sigh of relief. "She's gonna need you, Panda."

"She has me," I swear.

Austin's look is sympathetic, his blue eyes dark and

severe as he studies me. He flips his chin and I raise his phone.

"Code is 8215," he mutters.

I punch it in and the screen flares to life. I sit down on the bench, feeling like I just got the wind knocked out of me. Like a center plowed straight into me and pushed his stick against my throat.

Because my vision blurs and I suddenly feel like I can't breathe.

I scroll down the screen, each image of Abbi in a different provocative pose. Her breasts on full display, her hand between her legs, her mouth parted. Wild eyes, sexy lingerie, just-fucked hair.

I toss the phone on the bench beside me and lean forward, dropping my head.

What the fuck? "Who sent you these?" I demand.

"They're all over the internet."

Oh, shit. Puzzle pieces snap together in my head, comprising a whole damn puzzle of information. "I'm going to fucking murder Phil Rickens."

Austin nods in understanding.

"You knew?" I ask him. "About, about—" I glare at his phone.

"It's why she wanted to relocate. To start fresh after things at her last job…well, you know what happened."

"That's why you helped her secure this position?"

"Yes."

"And this is why you didn't tell me?"

Austin looks ashamed but he owns it. "Yes."

I shake my head. As much as I want to be angry with Austin, I can't help but feel thankful for him instead. "Thanks for looking out for her, Cap."

He frowns but nods at me. "Always."

"No, I mean it. I'm pissed at you for not telling me but I

get why you didn't. You put Abbi first and that's what I want for her. People having her back."

"Check your phone. Did she call you?" he wonders aloud.

I move to my locker and pull open the door, snatching up my phone.

I wince when I see all the messages from my family.

"Shit," I mutter, scanning them. "Seems these are making the rounds in Philadelphia too."

Austin curses. "She's linked to you so…"

I groan, dropping my head back. So of course her private pictures are fucking newsworthy. I've made this whole thing a million times worse for Abbi. It doesn't matter that I'd do anything to protect her. Because of my career choice, she's now being picked apart like a vulture, her naked photos circulating like a national phenomenon.

I keep scrolling, searching for her name. Disappointment kicks my stomach. "She didn't message me. Or call." I look at Austin.

"She's probably mortified."

"Yeah, well, she shouldn't be alone." I press her name and hold the phone up to my ear while it rings.

A second later, it cuts to voicemail.

"Her phone's off," I explain, frowning. Why didn't she call me? Why didn't she reach out to me?

"Chloe was going to pick her up from work," Austin says.

I nod, feeling a bit better that she's with Chloe and not off on her own somewhere. Still, I hate the fact that she ran to her friend first. Doesn't she know how much I care about her? Doesn't she realize how much I feel for her? That I'm always here for her?

"She had a really hard time after everything unfolded in New Jersey," Austin says and I narrow my eyes at him. While a part of me hates that he seems to know more about her experience there than I do, a part of me also wants to know everything he knows. So, I keep my mouth clamped closed and focus on Austin. "Phil did a number on her. And he came after Kent so…"

"Double whammy."

"Yeah." Austin cringes and walks toward me. "Look, I know things that Chloe told me in confidence. Right now, you need to be there for Abbi."

"I'm right here." I shake my phone at him, defensive as fuck.

"It's hard for her to trust. From what I gather, she trusts you, Panda. This is going to be hard for her and as angry as you are—" He holds up a hand as soon as I open my mouth. "Come on, how the fuck could you not be angry?"

I tip my head in acknowledgement.

"She needs you," he says.

"Do you know where they are?" I ask, hating how uncertain I suddenly feel when this morning, I would have sworn up and down that Abbi and I are a sure thing.

Then why didn't she call me? Why doesn't she need me? Or want me to help her through this?

Austin checks his phone. "Jolene's."

"Let's go."

"Want to head over together?" Austin asks and I glance at him, knowing he's toeing a thin line between being my friend and keeping Chloe's confidence.

"Sure," I accept.

"Come on, let's go get our girls."

I stand from the bench. "Let me shower and change really fast."

"Take your time. I'm sure they're not going anywhere. It's two-for-one margaritas today."

I groan, wondering what the hell I'm walking into.

CHAPTER 17
ABBI

"Margaritas are better than water," I trip over my words to Selina, the bartender.

"How do you figure?" She tips her head, her gaze sympathetic.

"They go down just as easy but have more of a…a zest, you know?" I blabber on, too miserable to be embarrassed for my rambling.

"I hear that, sis." Selina clinks her water glass against mine and takes a long pull on the straw. "I wish I was sitting on your side of the bar, tossing back tequila with you and your friend."

I look in the direction of the bathroom where Chloe loped off several minutes ago. I'd bet my life that she's calling Austin, which means, Luca will shortly know where I'm hiding out. I turn back to my colorful beverage, running my index finger through the salt on the rim.

Sighing, I meet Selina's eyes. "When's your shift over? I'm not going anywhere."

Her smile widens but she shakes her head. "I'm working a double. Heading over to Taps next."

I frown. "You work at two bars?"

"I work wherever I can make money. I'm an aspiring actress, keyword there is *aspiring*, so…whatever pays the bills." She shrugs, reaching for a shaker and more tequila. "Want to try a habanero one next?"

"Sure," I agree. "Just keep them coming."

"You got it," Selina says but I see her eyes cut to the other side of the bar. When I turn, I see Chloe and sigh. At some point, someone responsible is going to cut me off.

Good news? That someone doesn't have to be me. I drain my drink and push the empty glass in Selina's direction just as Chloe sits back down.

"How ya doing?"

I point to Selina, shaking up the margaritas. "We're moving on to habanero."

Chloe shakes her head. "Abbi, we have to think positively. This isn't the end of the world."

My mouth pops open, chagrin flooding my system. "It's the end of *my* world, Chlo. Everyone has seen my hoo-ha. And I do mean everyone."

"I haven't," Selina tosses out, placing two more margaritas down.

"Thank you for making that choice," I tell her truthfully.

Selina smirks. "Men suck."

"Tell me about it," I agree.

"But they're not all bad." She gestures toward Chloe. "Austin's a great guy and James treats my bestie, Bella, like a queen."

"True," I grumble, thinking about Luca. "Luca Pandatelli is the best man I know."

Surprise flares in Selina's eyes but she nods. "See?"

"But what will he think?" I nearly wail, the tequila hitting me now. My words slur softly, too many syllables colliding.

"That you're a strong, resilient woman, who was put in a compromising situation," Chloe explains rationally.

Selina nods and I feel my self-pity morphing into anger. Why doesn't anyone understand how humiliating this is? How I feel about two inches tall? How the thought of facing Luca, a man with a larger-than-life personality and too big heart, makes me feel like puking?

The door to Jolene's swings open and Selina's eyes widen. Chloe's hand settles on my forearm.

Without turning around, I know Luca just entered the bar. But I would have known even without Selina and Chloe's reactions. My body tightens and my nerves dance along my skin. I'm so in tune to Luca's presence, that I would feel him anywhere.

I drop my eyes closed and suck in an inhale, mentally preparing myself for his disappointment and disgust.

His hand wraps around the back of my neck, heavy and strong. My eyes fly open as I'm whipped backwards, barely able to steady myself, before Luca's lips descend on mine. His mouth is hot, his kiss intense. He kisses me with the simmering rage I feel surging just below my skin. He kisses me like he can absorb my pain and make it his. He kisses me hard, letting me know he's just as angry as I am but still…he's here.

"Let me get one of those, Lina," he orders, slipping onto the barstool beside me.

Austin shoots me a wink and a small smile before pulling Chloe down the bar, giving Luca and me some privacy.

"What are you doing here?" I turn toward Luca.

His eyes narrow as he studies me. "Was worried about you."

"I'm fine."

"You are," he agrees, nodding. "Thanks," he says to Selina. Then he taps the bottom of his glass against the rim of mine. "What are we drinking to?"

I narrow my eyes back. "What do you think?"

"Egotistical jocks with small dicks?"

I snort out a laugh, not expecting that.

"Or shitty liars who break vows?"

I dip my chin in confirmation.

"I know." He snaps his fingers. "The bullshit double standard that shames women while applauding men?"

I take a large gulp of my margarita.

"Cheers, baby." Luca takes a drink of his, placing his glass down on the bar. "You don't have to do this alone."

"Get drunk?"

"Any of it. Whatever you want to do, however you want to handle this, I'm in."

"You can't mean that." I roll my eyes to play off his words. But moisture floods my eyes at his kindness and something deep in my chest shifts. Who is this man? Can he be real? Can I trust it? Him?

A tenderness I've never seen before ripples over his expression. His lips part the tiniest bit, the tip of his tongue hitting his upper lip. He stares at me as if realizing, for the first time, just how deeply hurt and humiliated I feel. My heart is weary and sad. I've been wearing spiky edges, my tongue coated in barbs, as a protective shell for a long time. His fingers sweep my hair back, playing over the shell of my ear, brushing over the curve of my face. "Every goddamn word."

I frown, not following.

"I love you, Abbi Walsh. I mean every goddamn word I say to you. I don't give a shit about your past, baby, because I've got a past of my own. So however you want to play the present, count me in."

Selina's gasp rings in my eardrums like a gong.

My mouth falls open, my eyes widen, and my heart races. *He's for real.*

"Luca," I breathe out.

He gives me that lopsided grin I love and tugs me

forward, until I slip off the barstool, my feet hit the floor, and his knees cradle my frame, cocooning me. He kisses me again, hard and certain, as if the mess that is my life didn't scare him away.

As if we're unshakeable.

And I want to believe in that so badly that I close my eyes and kiss him back.

"SHE'S SLEEPING," Luca's voice wraps around my subconsciousness, gently tugging me from sleep.

I roll over in his bed, my head thrumming and my mouth drier than that Sahara. Margaritas. Shit.

I drop my hand on my face, rubbing my eyes open. I'm wrapped up in Luca's comforter and the door to his bedroom is ajar, the light from the living room flooding in.

What time is it? I grope around the bed for my cell phone as Luca speaks again. "Yeah, it was a rough day."

He sounds exhausted and a flicker of guilt shoots through me. I added more stress to his plate, when he's in the middle of hockey season and balancing all the things out for his family. I close my eyes again and rest my head back against the pillow.

"Fuck, man. Whatever you gotta do to get those photos down. I don't give a shit how much it costs or whose cock you need to suck. That's my girl and I'll be damned if fucking perverts across the country are gonna leer at her while they jack off."

I hiccup, laughter and disbelief and confusion rolling through me. I've seen charming, playful, endearing Luca Pandatelli before. I've even been introduced to tender, thoughtful, genuine Luca. But this version, serious, strong, and aggressive? I love that he's going to bat for me even though I didn't ask him to. I love that he cares enough to fight for me, even right now, when I'm not worth fighting for.

"Make it happen," he demands. Then, silence.

I'm about to pull myself from his bed when his phone rings again and he swears.

"What's up, Nikki?" Tiredness rounds out his words and I feel for him. How difficult it must be to be the man everyone needs? To show up all the time, for so many people? And now, to be the man I need on top of everything else?

"Shit," he murmurs, his voice low. I can picture him tipping his head back, his eyes closed. He sounds drained, emotionally and mentally fatigued, and I start to swing my legs to the side of his bed.

"No, I get what you're saying. Fuck, she wouldn't even be in this position if she wasn't linked to me. That's what sucks the most. If I didn't play hockey, or have some athletic career, those pictures wouldn't have blown up the way they did. I feel sick about it."

I falter, reaching out to steady myself on the corner of his nightstand. He feels guilty? About my photos? I bite down so hard, the copper taste of blood fills my mouth. This isn't on Luca; this is on me.

I stand, knowing I need to tell him as much, when his next words make me sit back down.

"Of course, we're still coming to Robbie's promotion dinner." A pause, followed by a swear. "I didn't even think of that. The guys are taking the piss? Fuck that. Look, as long as no one runs their mouths to Abbi, there won't be an issue. But if one fucker looks at her sideways, I can't promise they won't get my fist in their face."

I wince. Of course, my photos are all over Philadelphia. They're all over Boston and probably loads of cities and pretty much everywhere Internet exists in the U.S. I'm not saying it like it's an ego thing. For sure, I wish no one ever saw those images after Phil took them. I never should have let him take them. Or, at the very least, I should have deleted them afterwards.

But now, my vagina is everywhere and everyone is getting an up close and personal look.

I feel my cheeks flame at the thought. Poor Robbie is probably hearing an earload right now, as he prepares to step into a more senior position and accept a promotion. My stomach rolls as my embarrassment blazes.

My hands tremble and my head pounds as I lie back down. I can't go to Robbie's promotion. There's no way in hell I can walk into any type of public event with Luca by my side and embarrass the shit out of his family after he's done everything he can to keep them safe and healthy and cared for.

"Yeah, I know. I'll talk to her about it," Luca says from the other room.

Humiliation floods through me. His family is talking about me. No, they're talking about what to do *about* me. I'm nothing but a problem, a burden, an inconvenience to all who know me. If I wasn't, one would think that one of the men in my life would have stuck around these past thirty-plus years.

I blow out a shaky exhale, feeling mortified, angry, and yeah, a little sad for myself too. Luca is a good man and he shouldn't have to defend me to the nation and to his family.

"I'll talk to you later, Nik." He ends the call.

I hear him shuffle around in the next room. I roll onto my side and pull the comforter up over my shoulders. There's no way I can face him now. What would I even say? What the hell do I even want to do?

The door to his bedroom widens and more light floods in. I snap my eyes closed and feign sleep.

Luca approaches the bed, his footsteps quiet, his breathing even. His hand cups the side of my cheek, his fingers brushing lazily through my hair.

"We're gonna be okay, Abs," he whispers.

I keep my eyes shut, wondering if he's trying to convince me or himself.

CHAPTER 18
LUCA

The moment I skate onto the ice, I know I'm in for one hell of a game.

Firstly, because the Eagles are having a good season and are going to be a tough team to beat.

Secondly, because games with Vancouver always go sideways. Mainly because one of their players used to date Indy and the douchebag rubs it in Noah's face every chance he gets.

But tonight, there's going to be a third reason. Tonight, I'm hopped up on adrenaline and anger, a dangerous cocktail for a sporting event. My hands are itchy, desperate for a good fight. And the Eagles aren't known for keeping their mouths shut.

After several days of hell, fielding phone calls from my family, getting swept up into a social media and PR shitstorm, and battling it out on Abbi's behalf with senior management after they pulled the plug on her March break camps, a greeting muttered in the wrong tone will have me flying off the handle.

"You good?" Austin gives me a look as I glide in front of the net.

"Good," I confirm, lying through my teeth.

East shoots me a look over his shoulder and I know he sees through me. He narrows his eyes at me and I lift my chin, daring him to call me on it. He mutters something under his breath and turns away.

That's right. No one look at me sideways tonight. I don't have the patience, I don't have the practice, and I sure as fuck don't have the composure. Not when my girl's plastered across the Internet like some botched photo shoot gone wrong, some celebrity gossip turned sour.

I drop into position for the face-off and breathe a sigh of relief when Austin gains control of the puck, passing it to Noah who moves it up the ice.

Right now, I hold on to hockey, on to this game, with both hands. My head is fucked up, my body twisted, over everything Abbi is enduring. Work put her on a temporary leave of absence as they sort through the backlash her images have received from parents and school administrations around the city. She doesn't have any family to lean on. Chloe and I have been stepping up as much as we can but with both of us working and traveling, it's meant long, lonely hours for a vulnerable and hurt Abbi.

The puck travels down the ice in a whir of movement, hockey sticks, and massive, monsters of men. The Eagles winger tries for a shot on goal but I catch it, relieved I can still play the game with my head spinning in a hundred different directions.

I let my anger, my helplessness over this entire fucked-up situation, fuel me. My game is on point and while we score three goals by the third period, I don't let one shot pass into the net.

It's after a boarding penalty call that all hell lets loose.

James Ryan is pushed hard against the boards and Noah jumps in to push the Eagles center off-balance. Jace Edwards,

Noah's long-time nemesis, runs his mouth and the next thing I know, Easton's fist flies.

Finally. A surge of excitement, the first positive emotion I've felt all week, explodes through my limbs and I jump into the fray, cocking back my arm and letting my fist connect with one of the Eagles.

I hit one of their defensemen in the face but it's their right wing who pushes me over the edge.

"You can hit every guy on the ice and it won't change the fact that we've all jerked off to your girl's pussy," he taunts, his words callous. Dangerous.

Fighting words.

I turn and punch him in the mouth, smirking when blood shoots from his nose. He catches me across the face, making my anger surge into a blinding rage. I go all in on him, my fists flying, my chest heaving, my mouth running at full speed. He manages a few good hits and the fight turns ugly. The intensity is unmatched to any other altercation I've ever been involved in.

Shouts ring out, whistles pierce the air, but the sounds barely register.

"Lock your shit down," Austin growls as I feel arms cross over my chest like bands. A few more guys on both teams get in the middle to separate us, to quell the fighting.

My helmet connects with the boards. "Knock this shit off right fucking now," Austin's voice is murderous.

The guy I went at is lying in a heap on the ice, barely able to get to his feet. I look at him and feel sick. His face is a mangled mess. Streams of blood flow down his face and red tints his hair. I don't even know his goddamn name.

"Fuck," I mutter, realizing he's nearly unconscious. My hands shake as adrenaline leaves my body and disgust rushes in.

"Out," the ref boots me from the game.

Coach Phillips glowers and I feel sick to my stomach, bile

crawling up my throat as I stare at the player who finally manages to get his legs under him. One of his teammates grips him under the arm to support him and my shame nearly stamps out my existence. What the hell have I done?

"Get out of my sight," Coach tells me, not even looking me in the eyes. "I'll deal with you later."

I skate off the ice to the crowd booing. I can't bear to look at the box where the wives and girlfriends, the kids and families of players, sit. I can't witness the disappointment in any of their eyes.

So, I don't. I make my way back to the locker room, pull off my gear, and take a shower. When I'm fully dressed and seated in front of my locker, the door bangs open and the team files in. Even though we secured a win, no one looks happy. There's nothing to celebrate. Shame hangs over the locker room like a thundercloud.

And that's on me.

EVERY MOMENT SPENT in the company of anyone who isn't Abbi is like having bamboo sticks shoved under my fingernails. Torturous, painful, and awkward as fuck.

Coach suspended me from playing the next four games, which I deserved. The team is pissed at me, first for how I handled myself on the ice, and then for leaving them in a vulnerable position as we line up against tough opposition. Austin can barely look at me and I don't blame him. Only Easton, my teammate who wreaked his own kind of havoc a few seasons back, clutched my shoulder sympathetically and advised me to keep my head down until things blow over. But he promised things will eventually blow over. I'm not sure I believe him.

My family is worried, constantly calling to check in on Abbi and me. My sisters think I should skip Robbie's dinner since it's clear I can't keep my temper in check. Plus, they know I won't come without Abbi and they *know* things will suck for her if we show up together. Deep down, I know that too but their incessant calls and probing questions leave me with a bitter taste in my mouth.

That bitterness expands into shame when I recall that they watched me completely lose control. My nieces and nephews watched me pummel a guy with complete abandon. It's the kind of recklessness I swore I shook off years ago and yet, here I am, blistering with shame.

I feel wild, nearly unhinged with anger at myself and a need to do right by Abbi. To prove to her that I can be better.

Except, even Abbi is put out with me.

"You can't just blow off Robbie's dinner," she tells me one night over dinner. Her fork spears a piece of lettuce like it personally affronted her and the puffiness of her eyelids lets me know she's been crying.

Being suspended from her position, even though she did nothing wrong, rattled her. Having strangers gawk at her and yell out shitty, sexual things is messed up on every level. But now, even in the safety of our space, my apartment that I want her to think of as hers, the air is tight, the energy off.

All the external pressure and bullshit of the day-to-day follows us home every night, taking up residence in the space between us and making it seem like we're on opposite sides of a bridge, in the rain, when we're really only inches apart.

I blow out a heavy sigh. "This again? I'm not blowing it off, Abbi."

"So, you're going?"

"Yes."

"Good." The tines of her fork jab at a strawberry.

"With you," I add.

She rolls her eyes, her fork banging nosily off the rim of

her bowl when she drops it. "Luca, please. Why do we have to keep rehashing this? We're talking in circles. It's in everyone's best interest—mine, yours, *your brother's*—if I don't go to Philadelphia. Why won't you let this go?"

"Because you shouldn't have to hide," I bite out, my words severe. "You did nothing wrong. Why the hell should your life, our lives, be disrupted by some bullshit on the internet that trolls are getting off on? Why? Has anything changed for Phil? Let me guess, not a fucking thing." My fingers smack off the edge of the table as I push back my chair, ready to snap. "Why can't you see that?"

"I do see that!" she explodes, pushing her bowl away from her. "You don't think it kills me to know that this is all bullshit? That I'm in the middle of a freaking double standard? 'Oh, look at the slutty little home-wrecker. Let's all point our fingers at her for fucking athletes. She's got her hooks in a hockey player this time. Poor Phil, his wife is about to have a baby, and the family man doesn't need to deal with this drama'?" She changes her voice, mimicking gossip trolls. Tears gather in the corners of her eyes but they're an emotional overload from her anger, from the resentment that burns in her chest. And I'm happy to see them. I'll take this version of her, the fighting, kicking and screaming, tough girl over an indifferent one any day of the week.

"So, come to Philly. Don't let them dictate how you live your life."

She stares at me for a long second and then her shoulders roll forward, her face crumpling. "Don't you get it, Luca? I'm not going to win this. All I'm going to do is bring more negative attention to you and your family. You can't go around beating up every guy who talks shit about me. You're now *suspended* from playing."

"It's four games," I rationalize, even though guilt coats my throat.

"Four games," she scoffs, seeing through me. "Exactly. It's

four games," she emphasizes, holding up four fingers. "You're fighting with your team, your family, because of my stupid mistake. You're putting walls up between yourself and your people, the ones who've always had your back, because of *me*." Her voice cracks and she shakes her head. "Please, just go to your brother's dinner."

I sigh, scrubbing a hand over my face. "Abbi."

"I'm tired," she announces, standing from the table. She takes her half-eaten salad with her and tosses it in the trash. She stares at me from the kitchen, her eyes sad. "I'm going to head home tonight."

"Hey, come on." I stand up, holding out my arms. "We can figure this out. You don't have to run—"

"I'm not running."

"Or hide just—"

"I'm not hiding." Her tone is sharp. "I just, I'm tired. Okay?"

I stare right at her, witnessing the coldness that filters over her face like a shield. I understand why she's got her gloves on with the rest of the world, but why the hell is she still wearing them around me?

"Okay, baby," I murmur.

She shoots me a small smile that's fake as hell and mumbles good night.

I watch her walk away, wincing when the door latches behind her.

Growing up with two sisters, I'm a beast at navigating the emotions of women. For a guy who spent nearly two decades trying to get girls into my bed and not give the impression that it would mean anything, I'm a pro at reading the room.

But this room, this vibe, this woman is all new territory for me.

How can I keep her heart when she's got it locked up so damn tight?

CHAPTER 19
ABBI

Dry your eyes and straighten your spine.

Gran's voice rings in my ears as the water from the shower beats down on my head. It's hot and steamy and doing shit at hiding the fact that I'm sobbing. I know my eyes will be puffy and red and that Chloe will call me out when I meet her for lunch.

But why is everything spiraling? Why, after all the shit with Phil, and losing Gran, am I now losing Luca?

Because I can't keep him. Not when he's getting into it with his team, his family, his friends, because of my past. Not when he's blurring the lines between our relationship and his career. I can't let him sacrifice so much because I messed up, because I trusted the wrong guy, because I got played.

My fingertips press against the glass door as I try to regulate my breathing. Nothing about this past year has been easy. Except reconnecting with Luca. Shame on me for believing things could be so effortless. Haven't I learned by now that nothing is that simple? If it seems too good to be true, it's because it is.

I close my eyes and rinse the conditioner from my hair before stepping out of the shower. Going through the motions, I get ready for my lunch with Chloe. Now that I don't have an office to go to, now that my March camps have been postponed until summer, perhaps indefinitely, I have all day to wallow in my depressing thoughts. Chloe taking me to lunch is a power move. She wants to snap me out of my funk before she leaves for Central America next week. She'll be gone for two weeks as she writes a piece centered on child endangerment, trafficking, and migration.

Normally, I welcome Chloe's interventions. She's the only person, besides Gran, who I can count on. But now, I feel too exposed, too raw and hurt, to heed her tough love.

"Hey," I greet Chloe when she knocks on the door to my apartment.

"Hi," she replies, stepping inside. "Love what you've done with the place." She glances around my space.

I smirk. I haven't done shit with this apartment and it shows. Between moving in a whirlwind, desperate to leave Hoboken behind, and reconnecting with Luca, I haven't spent a lot of time here.

"Are we heading out or ordering in?" Chloe asks.

I narrow my eyes. "Just how tough is this tough love going to be?"

"Take a seat and we'll order something."

I groan, moving to my kitchen and grabbing two sparkling waters from the fridge. I slide one to Chloe while she taps on her phone.

"I'm getting us salads from that new place, The Leafy Green."

"Great," I say, popping the tab on my water and taking a sip.

I sit across from Chloe and watch as she places down her phone, settles her coat and purse on another chair, and fixes me with a stern look.

"Abbi Walsh."

"Chloe Crawford."

"I know what you're doing."

"No, you don't."

She lifts her eyebrows as if to ask, seriously?

I raise mine back and she smirks.

"You haven't been this salty in a long-ass time," she accuses me.

I snort, trying to keep my face blank but my emotions, a tumultuous, flowing river under the surface of my skin, rise to the surface.

"Why are you trying so hard to push him away?" Chloe's voice softens.

I scoff but she sees through me in a heartbeat.

"Why won't you let him in?" she tries again.

"He's going to bail."

"How do you know that?" Her eyes are pleading but her voice is even.

I exhale, glancing up at the ceiling to school my expression. "How can he not? He's already getting into it with his team, with his family, with everyone over me and these stupid pictures."

"That's his choice. His decision. He wants to support you. Why can't you let him?"

"I don't want him to put everything on the line for something that's so, so new…so fragile. Hell, I might not even be here next month."

Chloe frowns. "What do you mean?"

I gesture around my plain apartment, exasperated. "Chlo, I'm not even working."

"You're on a temporary leave."

"That could become permanent at any time."

"Abs, I feel for you. I really do. This is a shitty situation and Phil is a dick. But you can't let this shitstorm dictate everything."

I groan. "You sound just like Luca."

"Good. At least he's trying to talk sense to you."

"Moving here was a mistake. Letting Luca in was—"

"The right thing to do. He's crazy about you, Abbi. And you're in love with him."

My eyes shutter closed and a few tears leak out because…I am. I'm in love with Luca Pandatelli and all I'm offering him is heartache. And headaches.

"I can't go to Philadelphia with him. I can't meet his family like…like this." I point at myself, hot mess express over here.

The corner of Chloe's mouth ticks up. "Okay. Then tell him you're riding this one out but pick a date, a weekend, to go meet his family. He wants you to meet them. He's bringing you into his life, his world. Isn't this what you wanted?"

I nod, working a swallow. "But not like this."

"Like what?"

"Like the pathetic, naive—"

"Stop."

"Girl who everyone has seen naked."

Chloe shrugs. "At least you've got the goods."

I roll my eyes and plant my face down, my forehead resting against the edge of the table. "Chloe Ann, I'm…tired."

"I know. You haven't had a chance to get back on your feet before this next wave wiped you out."

"I miss Gran," I murmur, a quiet admission.

"She wouldn't want you to back down."

"I know," I say, knowing exactly what Gran would say if she was here.

Lift your head.

"You haven't mourned her yet," Chloe whispers.

I glance up and watch as the pieces click together in her mind. Her expression changes, her mouth twisting and her eyes softening.

"Abbi." Chloe extends her hand and my face falls.

Sobs wrack my chest for the second time today and I fold

in on myself. My best friend scurries to my side of the table, wrapping me up in a hug.

She's my last person. The last one I have that I can count on, that I know will show up.

What about Luca? my heart asks.

What about him? my head answers.

He's showing up.

For now.

"I'll end up ruining him," I tell Chloe.

She pulls back, her expression bleak. "You're not giving him a chance. You're not being fair."

I let out a huff, half humor, half tears. "What is fairness?"

Chloe lifts her eyebrows. "Turning philosophical, are we?"

I sigh and drag the backs of my hands across my eyes. "I don't know how to trust what's between us. I don't know how to trust him. Not after—"

"He didn't call."

"Yeah."

"And Phil betrayed you."

"There's also that," I agree.

"Not to mention Kent."

"Please don't."

Chloe snorts but her face reflects the pain I feel bleeding from mine.

"You've had a tough go of it, Abbi. And I don't have an answer for you. What I do know is in the past nine months since I've met Panda, I've never seen him look at a woman the way he looks at you. I've never seen him claim a woman the way he's claimed you. He's in love with you and he doesn't deserve to be punished for the mistakes the men before him made, any more than you deserve to be punished for them. So, stop punishing yourself."

Her words land hard, popping in my head like Pop Rocks. I grin when I think of my favorite childhood candy. Nothing in my life has ever been simple, and this seems no different.

"Do you really think I'm punishing myself?" I wonder aloud.

Chloe chews the corner of her lip, her green eyes sparking. "I think you're always skeptical of happiness, always waiting for the other shoe to drop. What if this time, it doesn't?"

"What if it does?" I counter.

"That's life, Abbi. And you said it yourself, what's fairness anyway?"

I snort out a laugh as a knock sounds at the door.

"I'll grab lunch; you get the plates," Chloe demands.

I nod, moving into the kitchen to pull out plates and cutlery.

We sit back down and open our salads.

"Mourn your gran," Chloe tells me.

"How am I supposed to do that?"

"Talk about her. Let yourself miss her. Share stories about her. Tell Luca about her. Does he even know that she raised you?"

I shrug. "A bit."

Chloe quirks an eyebrow. "Things between you and him can't blossom if you don't let him in, Abbi. You need to decide if you're going to make a real go of this or let it fade out the way—"

"I always do," I finish for her.

She shrugs, her eyes brimming with a sadness, an expectation, I don't like. It's as if I'm disappointing her and it hurts to know my best friend thinks I'm sabotaging my own relationship. Am I?

I tip my head, acknowledging the challenge in her eyes. "You're really going all in today, aren't you?"

"Tough love is real love," she answers, flashing me a grin. "And you're like a sister to me. I just want you to be happy."

"Yeah," I agree, lifting my fork to my mouth. "I'd like that too."

LUNCH WITH CHLOE puts a lot of things into perspective. I spend the remainder of the afternoon contemplating my relationship with Luca, thinking of Gran, remembering my childhood.

Mom passed when I was a kid, just on the peak of becoming a woman. Dad was already out of the picture, not even bothering to send child support payments as he took his new family to Disney World.

But Gran raised me as her own. She was both the mom and the dad and the grandmother. She was my shoulder to cry on, my number one cheerleader, and could rival a prison guard when necessary.

Losing her feels like I've lost a piece of myself. An important part that I don't know how to heal or recover now that Gran isn't here to tell me how.

I sigh and plop down on the couch, grabbing the remote control. I glance at the clock, knowing Luca should be home in another thirty minutes or so. I'm going to invite him over then, tell him about Gran, try to sort this next step out between us. Chloe's right; I'll never know what will happen if I'm not willing to try.

I frown as my face splashes across the television. What the hell? My eyes flick down to the bottom corner where the logo of a well-known celebrity gossip station lights up.

Well, well, well. No publicity is bad publicity.

I snort and turn up the volume, not entirely sold on that point.

"—linked to the lingerie model, Anastasia Luvorchik, who announced her pregnancy earlier this afternoon. She's naming Boston Hawks Hockey goalie, Luca Pandatelli, as the father. Most recently, he's in a relationship with Abigail

Walsh, the infamous woman allegedly breaking up happy relationships across the Northeast. Is this her latest work?"

Another image of me, an awful one, sloppy drunk in Luca's arms over the summer, appears on the screen and I gasp, my hand flying to my throat.

What the hell? Is Luca having a baby with, with a lingerie model?

My heart pounds, so loud I can hear it in my eardrums.

Is this a scandal? Did he know? Did he keep this from me?

Stop it. You don't know anything yet. You know what they say about those who make assumptions.

Yeah, but I've been made an ass of my entire life. Why should now be any different?

My phone buzzes next to me, the screen lighting up with an incoming call and a barrage of messages.

A lump forms in my throat and nausea rolls through me, twisting my stomach.

I need to talk to Luca. But now, I no longer want to.

CHAPTER 20
LUCA

"I can't get through," I holler, throwing my phone down. It skitters across the table before dropping to the floor. I let out a swear and turn, my fingers lacing behind my head, as I try to calm down. "How the fuck am I supposed to calm down?"

"We're going to fix this, Panda," my agent, Callie, says calmly.

I spin around and narrow my eyes at her. Her tone implies that I'm throwing some toddler temper tantrum when, "I have every right to be upset right now. That's not my baby." I point at the television where stupid gossip fodder is spinning a web of damaging lies. Not just damaging to me and my career, but damaging to my brother, my family, and most of all, to the woman I'm in love with.

Hell, I am so damn in love with Abbi. She's not going to want me now. Not when I'm embroiled in a scandal while she's battling one of her own.

I pinch the bridge of my nose and swear. Slipping into the chair across from Callie, I accept my phone from her hand and mutter a thank you. "What do we do?"

"Well, our first step is to shut this shitstorm down—" She

flicks her wrist toward the television at large where images of me, looking like the playboy I was, flicker across the screen. "Then, we'll work on proving you're not the father. We'll need to do a paternity test. We're going to launch a serious PR campaign. We need to show you as a family man now more than ever."

"My family stays out of this."

Callie sighs but doesn't push. "You want to make a deal with her?" She glances at the television, even though it's now turned off. If I have to see Anastasia's face one more time… "Girl's looking for a pay day. It could be the fastest way to make this go away."

"Not a chance in hell. I am not the father and I'm not going to pay some woman off to stop spreading lies. She's lying." I jab my finger at the black television screen.

Callie nods, her eyes snapping to mine. The familiar fire that has made her such an ass kicker in this industry, flares to life. Her ambitious, badass energy soothes me and I know she's going to straighten this out for me. I lean back in my chair, my fingers tapping on the table. "I don't care about all this." I gesture around. "I just want Abbi. And now, she's not speaking to me."

Callie's expression softens. "You really care about her, huh?"

I snort, scrubbing my face again. God, I'm tired. Drained really. But I have a game tonight, my first game back, and I need to snap out of this unproductive headspace and show up ready to play. "I love her," I tell Callie, staring right at her.

She rears back slightly, surprise widening her eyes. But after a moment she smiles and for the first time since I've met her, she looks pretty. I mean, to most men, Callie James is a smoke show, but around here, she's more of a barracuda, and I'd be lying if I said I wasn't scared of her. "Good for you, Panda. Really."

"Cal, she won't speak to me," I state slowly, reminding her of the problem.

Callie rolls her eyes. "She will. Give her time. This lifestyle is overwhelming if you're not used to it. It's a lot up front and she's dealing with her own stuff. She could be overloaded, trying to process."

"I thought that's the messed-up shit guys do."

Callie laughs and stands from her chair. "Maybe I'm giving you bad advice. I've always been accused of thinking too much like a man. Too rational, not feeling enough."

I shake my head. "No way. That's what makes you a boss at your job."

She shoots me a grateful smile. "Maybe. But it also makes me single in my forties."

I scoff, disliking that Callie is letting me see a chink in her armor. Not because she trusts me with a personal piece of herself, but because there shouldn't be a damn chink. Not when it comes to her dating life. A woman like Callie deserves the world and I tell her so.

"Ahh"—she shakes her head—"behind that reputation, you really are too good, Pandatelli."

"Yeah, well don't go spreading that around." I point to the conference room door.

Callie chuckles. "I'll keep it close to the vest. I'm going to get started on the Anastasia issue. You track down your girl and focus on your game tonight." She points at me, all stern and serious again. "Don't let this drama affect your play. It's your first game back on the ice and several of your endorsements are shaky. Don't give the sponsors a reason to pull them. I know there's a lot going on, but you still need to do your job. You've gotta show up the way we all know you're capable of. Got it?"

I slap my palm against the table and straighten. "Got it. Keep me posted on what's what."

"Talk soon, Panda."

Callie leaves the conference room, but I sit for a minute, staring out at the Boston city streets beyond the floor-to-ceiling windows. From here, I can see the airport and the reminder that I'm flying to Philly, to my brother's promotion ceremony and dinner, in under forty-eight hours, pierces me. Is my bullshit going to overshadow his achievement?

I was such an idiot, acting like I was untouchable. For years, too many seasons, I acted with impunity. I really believed that I had cracked the code with women. Be upfront, be funny, make them have a good time, and there'd be no hard feelings.

Anastasia and I hooked up once. It was months ago, after a big win against Chicago. I was a little tipsy on tequila and riding the natural high from saving the puck against a buzzer-beater tie. Ana looked like she stepped off the cover of a lingerie magazine, all curves and long hair. She smelled delicious, purred in my ear, and made me feel like I was bigger, better, than every other guy in the room.

I caved. It was one night. And, to be honest, it wasn't even that good of a night. She was a fake moaner and I was desperate to be done with it all and bounce. If I knew the headache hooking up with her would cause, I wouldn't have touched her with a ten-foot pole.

I push back from the table and stand, walking over to the window. I stare out until I find the waterfront building where Abbi lives. She's there now, ignoring me, probably wishing she never tangled up with me in the first place.

Anastasia Luvorchik may have the modeling career and the type of beauty that women think defines desire.

But Abbi Walsh has the natural curves that get me hard the moment I see her. She has the type of mind that challenges and inspires me. Not to mention her heart is the only one I've ever wanted to sync up with. Abbi is the woman of my dreams and right now, she's not giving me the time of day.

"Panda." A knock sounds out a second after my name is called.

I turn around, frowning when I see James Ryan, our defenseman, in the doorway.

"You good?" he asks, frowning at me.

"Yeah," I say, yanking on the back of my neck. "What are you doing here?"

"Quick meeting with Nick." He points down the hall where his agent, Nick Stansela, holds meetings at The Meadows.

I nod and move toward him. "Right."

"Hey." He grabs my forearm when I'm closer. "All of this will eventually blow over. In another week, this will be old news. It'll be like it never happened."

"Sure," I agree, forcing a smile. But inside, my stomach clenches and I feel sick. Because while James is right, this will blow over, he's also wrong. In another week, I could lose Abbi forever.

I won't ever forget that we happened. If only for a moment.

"WHERE IS SHE?" I corner Chloe as soon as the game ends and I'm able to slip past the press, all clamoring for a statement when, for once in my life, I have nothing to say.

"Take it easy, man," Austin says, a warning clear in his tone.

I sigh, scrubbing a hand over my face. "I'm sorry, Chlo. I'm just, I'm worried about her."

Chloe nods in understanding, her expression softening as she places a hand on my forearm. She steers me away from the friends and family waiting for players, into a quiet corridor.

"What is it?" I whisper, knowing Austin is close behind.

"Panda, she's got a lot going on right now."

"What does that mean?" I work to keep my voice controlled. The last thing Chloe needs is my misplaced anger but damn, now my concern is morphing into frustration because—is Abbi letting her girl give me the brush-off?

Chloe sighs and fiddles with the ends of her hair. Austin steps up beside her, his hand finding her hip protectively. "It means, she's not in a good headspace right now. She's working through things and …"

"And?"

"She needs time." Chloe's voice is filled with apology but her words still rip through me.

"So, she's letting you speak for her now? How the hell can she shut me out like this?"

Chloe wrings her hands together, shuffling from one foot to the next. "Please try to understand. She's struggling—"

"With?"

Helplessness fills Chlo's eyes but I don't give a damn. I want answers. And even though it's not fair to put Abbi's best friend, my Captain's girl, on the spot, that's exactly what I do.

"I can't tell you that," Chloe murmurs. "She needs to tell you. And honestly, I don't know if she's at a place where she can. Yet."

As quickly as my anger spiked, it transforms into concern. "Is she okay?"

"I hope so," Chloe murmurs.

"Chloe, what the hell—"

"Sorry. Physically she's fine. She's not in danger or anything," Chloe blurts out.

"Well thank fuck for small miracles," I shoot back.

Austin shoots me another warning look, pulling Chloe back against his chest.

"Sorry," I mutter again.

Chloe gives me a soft smile. "I know you're worried. It's just, Abbi's working through a lot of things right now, Panda. She feels guilty about you being suspended. She's ashamed that those photos leaked. She's…look, she has a tough time letting people in." I open my mouth to point out how easily she clicks with Chloe's friends and the Boston girls, but Chloe holds up her hand. "She's friendly and warm and kind. She's an amazing friend who always gives an ear or a shoulder. But she doesn't let people in to be there for *her*. Abbi and I were friends for years in college but it wasn't until she got played by her college boyfriend—"

"Kent," I spit out.

"Kent." Chloe nods. "It wasn't until Kent and the drama that unfolded in the sorority house that Abbi really let me in. I had been trying for two years and while we were close, we were always discussing my drama or issues, and only glossing over hers. It took a life-shifting event that left her hurt and reeling for her to turn to her closest friends, to really trust me. She opened up to you faster than I've ever seen before and I think even that scares the hell out of her." Chloe tucks her hair behind her ears and shoots me an apologetic smile. "Right now, she's safe but she's working through some things and that's all I can tell you. If she wants to talk, she'll reach out. But if she's not taking your calls, it's best to back off for a minute."

"Back off?" I repeat, staring at the adorable couple before me. Suddenly, I'm angry at them. How dare they give me advice when they're cuddled up looking like an engagement photo shoot?

Austin sighs, reaching forward to clasp my shoulder. "Give it a few days, buddy. Just, go to Philly tomorrow, spend time with your family, and let the dust settle."

At his words, horror rolls through me. "You mean because of Anastasia?"

"I mean because of a lot of things," he says.

I shake off his touch and mumble good night under my breath.

Then I head home to an empty apartment that seems to close in on me as I realize just how alone I am. The next morning, I avoid the Internet at all costs and board a plane to Philly, wondering if Abbi will ever speak to me again.

I don't have to wonder long because when I land, all hell breaks loose, and I hate myself for putting my girl in such a vulnerable position.

"Pandatelli, are the rumors true?"

"Are you about to become a baby daddy?"

"How's Abbi taking the news? Or is she upset you didn't knock her up first?"

"Are you going to support your child?"

"Where's Abbi?"

Paparazzi and reporters alike swarm. Cameras flash, blinding me. My anger rises but this time, I have the good sense to swallow it down. I duck my head and move through the bodies blocking my path to baggage claim.

"What? You're not going to talk to us? Come on, Panda, give us something."

"You used to smile more. This girl is really messing with your head."

"Any words to Timms?" one of them hollers, mentioning the guy I pummeled. I wince and pull my suitcase off the belt.

Luckily, two men flank me moments later and point toward the exit. They're dressed in suits and I'm not sure if they're security, a car service, or fancy bloggers.

"What's going on?" I ask, as one of them reaches for my suitcase.

"Callie sent us," he explains. "We got a car waiting for you right there." He points to the windows, and I see a black sedan with tinted windows idling at the curb.

Relief rolls through me. "Thanks, guys."

I follow them to the exit, grateful for their presence as the paparazzi and reporters fall back a bit. They still yell out taunts and questions but they're easier to ignore now that they're not in my face.

Once I'm seated in the car and we're pulling away from the airport, I dial Callie.

"You okay?" she answers.

"That was fucking mayhem," I bite out.

"I figured it would be crazy. Did you see the headlines?"

I pinch the bridge of my nose. "No. Now what?"

"Anastasia is claiming that you knew about her pregnancy from the beginning but refused to engage with her."

"That's bullshit! She fabricated this whole thing."

"I know that, and you know that," Callie says calmly. "But to everyone else, it looks…"

"Like I'm a worthless, piece of shit guy who thinks with my dick," I finish the sentence.

Callie clears her throat and I swear.

"Callie, forget about me for a second. My girlfriend is being portrayed as a home-wrecker, an athlete chaser who will spread her legs for any man who wears a jersey, when—"

"I'm doing everything I can to fix it."

"Well, try harder. Please."

"I'll keep you posted, Panda. Right now, try to enjoy this time with your family."

I snort humorlessly and she laughs with me. It's a release of tension.

"This is pretty fucked up," I comment.

"It's a fucking shitstorm," Callie agrees. "Right now, I'm reaching out to Anastasia's team. Maybe we can work some-thing out."

"It's not my baby," I remind her, knowing in my gut that I'm not the father.

"We still need to prove that with a paternity test," my agent says gently. "Let me make some calls and I'll check in with you later."

"Okay. Thanks for...sending these guys." I wave toward the two men sitting in the front of the car.

"No problem. Keep your head tonight. No matter what anyone says—"

"Don't knock them out?"

"Don't give them the time of day," she says with finality.

"Yeah. Talk to you later, Callie."

"I'm serious, Panda."

"Me too." I disconnect the call and watch Philadelphia streak past through the window.

I know what's waiting for me at Pop's house. I can easily conjure up the concerned and disappointed expressions of my sisters, the worried twist of Robbie's mouth, the pain in Jenni's eyes. Again, humiliation and guilt burn through me. Squeezing my eyes closed, I force myself to consider the damage control I need to do with my family, even though I'd rather think about the beautiful brunette who won't take my calls.

CHAPTER 21
ABBI

"You need to hear him out," Chloe advises, nudging my colorful beverage closer.

I ignore her, picking up the cocktail and sucking down an unhealthy amount of tequila. Damn, Austin made these margaritas strong. I turn toward him as he moves to exit the kitchen, and raise my drink in a silent salute. He shoots me a sympathetic grin before he turns the corner into the living room.

"Abs, I'm serious," Chloe tries again. She ducks her head to catch my gaze and concern colors her jade eyes.

"I don't want to hear anything else," I reply, as if that settles the issue.

Chlo lifts an eyebrow.

"What is he possibly going to say?" I toss my hand in her direction, waiting for her to say something that clears Luca's name from being the baby daddy in the newest drama plaguing the NHL.

If my name—as a home-wrecker—wasn't in everyone's mouths, and if the baby daddy in question wasn't Luca, I'd be happy that a new issue has captured the nation's attention. Instead, I feel even worse than I did last week. Somehow, this betrayal strikes deeper, making me feel cheap on top of naive. How could he not tell me he fathered a child? How could he not tell me he got serious with a woman since last summer?

"He may not even be the dad!" Chloe argues, throwing a hand back in my direction.

I give her a look that says "I wasn't born yesterday," and she glares back at me.

"How can you, a person who has been on the receiving end of twisted, negative, exploitative gossip judge so harshly?" Chloe demands.

"Damn, you're going all in today." I take another gulp of my margarita.

"Abbi, you're jumping to conclusions without even giving Panda a chance to explain. How would you feel if he did that to you?"

I sigh and hang my head. Deep down, I know she's right. I am being judgey. But I'm also being smart, right? Protecting myself, my heart, from inevitable heartbreak. Isn't it better things fall apart now than in a few more months, when I'm in even deeper? My mom's face, haggard and hurt, the day my father walked out on us flares to life in my mind, and I close my eyes against it. No matter how much progress I make, it seems like all my downfalls hinge on that awful moment.

"I'd feel terrible, Chlo," I admit, forcing myself to meet her eyes. "But I'd also feel terrible if it turns out that Luca is about to become a father. A *father*. I can't bear the thought that he'd walk away from that obligation, away from his kid."

"He wouldn't."

"How do you know that? If I'm in the picture, horrified that he's having a baby with another woman? And I feel like complete shit that everyone in America thinks I'm some type of perpetual home-wrecker. I feel like crap that Luca's going to see his family this weekend and all everyone is going to talk about is the slutty girl with the slutty pictures that he's dating, instead of focusing on his brother's well-deserved promotion. So really, no matter which way I look at it, I'm going to feel like complete shit."

Chloe's expression softens, empathy flaring in her eyes. "You should still hear him out," she whispers.

I shrug, downing the last of my drink. "Maybe when I'm in a better headspace."

"Okay," she agrees, nodding. "I get it; you need time."

"I need more than that."

Chloe raises her eyebrows, waiting for my response.

"I'm going home," I announce, the idea just popping into my head. It's spontaneous but the second I say the words, I realize how much I need to be somewhere familiar. I need Gran.

"What?" Her mouth drops open. "No, you can't just run away every time—"

"I'm not running. At least, not away from my problems. I'm running toward them."

"I don't understand."

"I never said goodbye to Gran. Not properly. I never confronted Phil. Or Kent. I never got any of the closure I need to do this…" I gesture around her apartment.

"What is this?" Chloe mimics me.

I sigh. "Life."

My best friend smirks.

"I need to handle my shit before I hear Luca out. And to be honest, I don't even know how to do that."

"Want some company?" Chloe offers. I can tell by her tone that she means it and emotion swims in my eyes. "Hey." She reaches out, covering my hand.

My face falls and I squeeze my eyes shut to stop the tears that rush forward. In a world where I am totally on my own, it's a miracle to have a friend like Chloe Crawford.

"You'd really do that?"

Chloe's face mirrors mine. "Of course. Abbi Walsh, you're my person. It's always me and you. I love you more than a sister. Why do you think I'm trying so hard to make sure you don't have regrets with Panda?"

I hiccup and we stare at each other before we burst into laughter. At the emotional overload, tears streak down my face along with snot. It's probably one of my most unattractive moments but I don't care because it feels good to laugh. It feels right to be with my best friend. I feel like I catch my footing a bit and even though I'm definitely stumbling, I'm not free-falling.

"Let's go to Hoboken," Chloe says, pulling out her phone. "Let me sort some things out with work. I'm sure I can work from the New York office for a few days before I fly out." She raises the phone to her ear.

"And I'm on temporary suspension so..."

Chloe shakes her head, pointing at me. "Think of it as a blessing. Now you have time to take care of the things that need taking care of. For your own sanity, for your future. Hey, Janie." She turns away as her boss answers the phone.

As Chloe sorts things out for our impromptu trip back to the place where it all started—our friendship, my life with Gran, my struggle with men—I pull out my phone.

My heart rate kicks up when I see Luca's name on the screen. I scroll passed the three missed calls from him and scan the messages.

LUCA

Abs, I get that you don't want to talk to me. Just, please, let me know you're okay? I can explain everything if you give me the chance. Please, baby. Just give me five minutes.

LUCA

Abbi, I'm boarding a flight for Philadelphia. Please check in with me? Just a text?

LUCA

> I'm here. My family is ripping me a new one for being so careless. For hurting you. I know you're hurting, Abbi. But I swear, the baby isn't mine.

LUCA

> Talk to me. Please.

My throat burns as I read his messages. He's not the father? How can he be so sure? Chloe told me how he showed up to Austin's awards dinner in September with a beautiful brunette on his arm. She sure as hell wasn't Anastasia Luvorchik so how many women have there been? Can I trust his words? Just accept them at face value?

I did that with Kent. And Phil. It wasn't until I physically saw them with other women that I realized what a fool I was for blindly believing the lies that fell from their mouths.

But Luca isn't Phil. Or Kent. Deep down I know that.

Besides, I'm not the same woman with Luca that I was with my exes.

My stomach twists, the tequila sloshing around as the buzz I've been riding all afternoon pushes me into nearly drunk girl territory. I'm all over the place. Still, guilt squeezes my chest as I read Luca's messages again. He's now with his family in Philadelphia. His loud, meddling, adoring family and they somehow care about me, even though I'm blowing up Luca's life. Even though they never met me.

But he wanted them to. He invited me home. Home.

I don't know what that feels like anymore but I want to. With him.

Sighing, I tap out a reply.

ABBI

> Hi. I'm fine but I'm not ready to talk. Enjoy the weekend with your family.

He replies quickly, startling me.

LUCA

Are you just saying that? Because I'm not
fine.

ABBI

I'm not fine either.

LUCA

Where are you?

ABBI

Chloe's

LUCA

I swear I'm not about to become a father.

ABBI

Are you one-hundred percent certain?

The bubbles appear at the bottom of the screen before disappearing. My stomach sinks. He doesn't know. He *wants* to believe he knows the answer, but he doesn't.

LUCA

We're doing a paternity test.

My throat dries and a wave of nausea rolls over me.

Luca might have a baby with a supermodel. And here I am, gulping back margaritas, while the entire nation thinks I'm a serial screwer of taken men.

My father flits to mind and for the tiniest flicker, I feel a moment of sympathy for him. That maybe he made some mistakes and found himself in a compromising position. But then that feeling morphs into disgust as I remember how horribly he handled everything that came after. No, he should have been a father first and a husband, partner, lover second. And that's what Luca should be now. Before he can even consider having a future with me, he needs to learn if he's going to be dad. Because above all, his obligation should be to that child.

I drop my head into my hand and breathe in gulps of oxygen. I can't do this. Not with him and not right now.

My phone vibrates in my hand and when Luca's name appears on the screen, I decline the call.

He texts a moment later.

LUCA

Talk to me, Abbi. Please.

I stall, wondering what I should say.

LUCA

Please, baby. I need to know where your head's at.

I let out a slow exhale, tuning in to Chloe's voice as I get a handle on my emotions.

ABBI

Honestly? I'm struggling. I need some time. And space. Just, enjoy the weekend with your family and we'll talk soon.

He calls again and again, I decline.

LUCA

Abbi, don't shut me out like this. I know things are complicated but I'm all in with you.

ABBI

Go celebrate your brother, Panda.

LUCA

Panda? So that's it? You're going to write me off because of bullshit gossip? You of all people know how twisted things can get.

Tears pinch the corners of my eyes. He's right, just the way Chloe is. But I'm terrified. How can things ever go back to normal between us? Especially now, when we're both in the center of scandals, with our names being dragged through the mud? Across the table, Chloe watches me cautiously.

LUCA

Stop pushing me away. I'm not going anywhere.

ABBI

I'm not pushing. I'm pulling away. Please, respect my wishes.

After that, I power off my phone and toss it in my bag.

"You good?" Chloe asks.

I shake my head. "Not even a little."

"Babe," my best friend sighs. "Tell me what you want to do."

"I want to see Gran," I admit the truth, not caring if it makes me look weak. *Dry your eyes and straighten your spine.* "Take me home, Chloe."

She nods. "We leave in the morning. Come on, you're staying with me tonight."

I pull my hand back, shaking my head. "No. I can't stay here with you and Austin and—"

"We're sleeping at Mom and Dad's," she cuts me off, shooting me an understanding smile. "Mom's already cooking dinner and sent Dad out to buy the wine you like."

"The good stuff," we say at the same time and I smile.

"You're sure?" I ask again.

"Positive, Abs. I got you."

I nod, biting my bottom lip. I wait until Chloe talks to Austin and packs a weekend bag. Then, I let her drive me to her parents' house and I sink into Mrs. C's warm embrace, relishing the hug that only a mother can give.

"You're going to be okay, sweet girl," Mrs. C. whispers.

Dry your eyes and straighten your spine.

"I hope so," I murmur back because right now, it doesn't feel like it.

CHAPTER 22

LUCA

Nikki's the first to pull me into a hug and when she does, some of the tension I've been carrying around like stones dissipates.

"I'm so sorry," my sister murmurs.

I shake my head and pull back, staring into her worried eyes. "I'm fine."

"Bullshit," Robbie says, clapping me on the back. "Unless you're not really in love with Abbi?"

"What?" I whirl on him, frowning. "Of course, I'm in love with her. All fucking in."

My brother lifts an eyebrow. "Then you're definitely not okay."

"But we have booze," Justine calls out, coming over to kiss me hello. "Pop even broke out the scotch. Says you earned it."

I snort. "Me being kicked to the curb, lying in the gutter, has finally earned me the scotch? Not winning the Stanley Cup or anything?"

Robbie chuckles as my sisters shrug.

"Good scotch is only for the best and worst moments," Dad says, hobbling into the room. I move toward him but he swats me away, fixing me with a sharp look. "The best and worst moments are always and only with the one you love. Nothing else really matters, or ever comes close, to those."

I tip my head, conceding his point. He settles into a chair and looks me up and down. "Besides, you look like shit."

Robbie snickers and moves to the bar to pour me a glass of scotch. When my brother passes it to me, I turn to Pop. "Can we at least toast to Robbie's promotion?"

A swell of pride washes over my brother's face. My step-mom, Jenni, kisses the top of my head, and helps Robbie pass out a round of drinks.

Pop swears, muttering about how I still don't get it, but Justine lifts her glass. "To Robbie, our fearless brother. We are so proud of you."

Robbie dips his head but I see the gratitude that sparks in his eyes.

"You deserve this, man," I tack on.

"Thanks for coming, Luca," he says, taking a slow sip of scotch.

"Wouldn't miss it. It's about time the Pandatellis have something good to celebrate."

"You dating a woman counts." Nikki points at me, taking the piss.

I flip her the middle finger and Justine laughs.

"So, are we gonna talk about it now?" Robbie lifts his eyebrows.

"Talk about what?" I ask, sitting up straight. Did something happen? Is Valentina's bronchitis back? Are one of my nephews in trouble?

"You getting your head out of your ass and winning the girl back," Pop explains, artful as ever.

"What?" My mouth drops open.

"We've never seen you like this," Jenni says, sitting next to Pop. She slips her hand in his and he squeezes, brushing his thumb over her knuckles. It's such a simple gesture but it speaks to years together, to mutual respect, to celebrating the highs and weathering the lows. It speaks to scotch drinking.

"We really thought you were going to bring her," Justine says softly, perching on the edge of the couch. "I'm sure this is hard on her but we're your family, Luca. You guys shouldn't be alone trying to sort all this media stuff out."

"She went home," I say, clearing my throat.

"Where's that?" Nikki asks.

"New Jersey. Her gran passed and—"

"Oh, that poor girl." Jenni lifts a hand to her mouth.

"No, not right now. She passed in November and—"

"She needs closure," Justine says knowingly.

I frown. "What?"

"There's just too much happening in her life," Nikki continues, as if I'm not sitting here, trying to understand what the hell is happening. And why does my family always hijack a conversation and run with it? They don't even know Abbi. "When things get tough, the first thing you want is—"

"Home," Jenni murmurs.

"The familiar," Justine agrees.

"Comfortable," Robbie adds, getting into this.

"It must be so hard for Abbi, in a new city, with a new job, new relationship"—my sister-in-law, Robbie's wife Nella, glances at me—"and now all of this."

"She needs time," Nikki confirms, nodding.

"We understand why you didn't bring her." Justine looks at me.

I scrub a hand over my face, trying to keep up. "Okay."

"But you should really go get her," Nella adds.

I drop my hand and look up. "To New Jersey?"

"Wherever she is." Nella shrugs. "She needs to know that you're going to show up for her."

"I'm being accused of impregnating a woman with a child who isn't mine," I remind my family, starting to grow frustrated with how they're all suddenly relationship experts.

"Abbi's name is being dragged through the mud because of my stupid decisions. She doesn't want to talk to me."

"Probably not," Nikki agrees. "But she still needs you."

"She's not talking to me," I spell it out for them, dragging a hand through my hair. I'm agitated. Doesn't my family realize how much I miss my girl? How much I wish she was here with me, right now?

"So, make her," Pop says, as if that settles it.

I narrow my eyes at him and he narrows his right back at me.

"Is she the woman you drink scotch over?" He lifts an eyebrow, pissing me off.

I down my glass and smack my lips together.

Pop grins. "Then go to New Jersey. Get your woman. And bring her home to meet your family."

"We really can't wait to meet her," Nikki gushes.

"You guys are crazy," I mutter, standing from my chair. I point to my brother. "I'm not missing your dinner. But tomorrow, I'll, I'll head to Hoboken."

Justine squeals and Nella smiles.

"If she'll still have me, I'll bring her to the next family event," I say, the pressure in my chest easing as I speak the words aloud. God, I hope Abbi will still have me. I smirk at my family. "You're all massive pains in my ass."

My family laughs as the door opens and the herd that is my nieces and nephews tumbles in.

"Uncky!"

"Hey, Uncle Luca."

"Missed you," Laura rushes me, raising her arms.

I swing her up into my arms, even though she's getting way too big for that, and lay a loud kiss on her cheek. "Missed you, ladybug."

"Are you having a baby?" she asks, her eyes wide.

My stomach sinks but I keep my face blank as I shake my head. "No."

"Do you still have a girlfriend?" Gino asks.

"I hope so," I say honestly.

"You need to do something special for her," Jack advises, looking well beyond his twelve years.

"Is that right?" I shoot Justine a look. She rolls her lips together, trying not to laugh.

"Yep. But Mom says girls don't like it when you annoy them just because you like them," he continues.

"It's outdated," Gino adds seriously.

This time, I chuckle. "So, what should I do?" I ask the little horde of fart faces I love like my own kids.

"Prove that she can trust you," Jack says.

"A pony," Valentina suggests.

"Nope." Laura shakes her head. "Buy her a ring."

"And ask her to marry you!" they all shout in unison.

My sisters and brother chuckle but I freeze because where that statement would have sent me spiraling a year ago, it doesn't make me panic the way it used to.

"Luca, he's kidding," Nikki says.

"I know," I say, biting the corner of my lip.

"Holy shit," Robbie mutters, earning a smack from his wife for swearing in front of the kids. Not that they haven't heard it before.

"Get my son another scotch," Pop calls out.

Then my family laughs, my sisters wrap me up in hugs, and I nod as Robbie books me a train ticket to Newark, New Jersey for Sunday morning.

BEING with my family grounds me the way it always does. I remember my roots; I remember who I am and what I want. And I want Abbi Walsh.

But while I've been in Philadelphia, surrounded by a flock of family who always has my back, I can't help but think who's looking out for Abbi? Yeah, she has Chloe who is one hell of a friend. But she doesn't have the home you can always show up at and know you'll be welcomed. She doesn't have the history with a group of people who love you, even at your worst. She doesn't have that safety net and I wonder if that's why she always runs and hides? Why would she give her trust when no one, save for Chloe and the Crawfords, have ever kept it safe for her? Can she ever truly trust me? Confide in me and allow me to be the man, the family, she leans on?

After a pretty special weekend celebrating my brother's achievements, I kiss my munchkins goodbye and board a train to New Jersey. The two-hour ride leaves me with plenty of time to sort out what I want to say to Abbi.

That I received a phone call early this morning from Callie, confirming that I'm not the father. Even though we're still waiting for the paternity test results, the real father stepped forward, claiming his rights as a dad. And with the financial support that followed, Anastasia admitted the truth. Her pregnancy doesn't match up with the date of our hooking up. Her team will release a statement today, clearing Abbi's and my names from the drama of hers.

Then, Callie promised she will do everything she can to spin a more positive message surrounding Abbi and her outreach work. I know it won't solve everything overnight but it's a step in the right direction. While I'm not too concerned with my reputation, I don't want my poor decisions to affect Abbi's.

"How's it going?" A man sits down next to me.

"Hey," I say, lifting my chin in greeting.

"Traveling for business or pleasure?" he asks, narrowing his eyes at me. I can tell he recognizes me but can't place me. It's a bit of a relief he doesn't know exactly who I am.

In fact, it fills me with a lightness, an ease, to admit the truth. "Trying to win my girl back."

He leans back, surprised by my honesty. Then he chuckles, and shakes his head. "How badly did you mess up?"

"Pretty bad," I admit, glancing out the window.

"Cheat on her?"

"No."

"Lie to her?"

"Nope." I shake my head, turning back toward him.

He studies me. "Drugs, alcohol, gambling?"

"None of the above."

He nods and pulls EarPods out of his bag. "Then you'll be fine."

"How do you know?"

"If you're traveling on a train on a Sunday to apologize for something you didn't even do, she'll forgive you. Women love a grand gesture. And taking SEPTA to NJ Transit is pretty damn big."

I laugh but he shoots me a knowing glance.

"You're serious?" I ask, wondering how low women's standards for a grand gesture are. Taking public transportation shouldn't rate that high.

"Trust me," he says, popping in an EarPod.

"Okay," I say, deciding to take him at his word. Leaning back in my seat, I watch the outside pass by, counting down the minutes until I can apologize to my girl.

And hopefully, bring her home.

CHAPTER 23
ABBI

I spent the day brunching and shopping in Hoboken with Chloe. We visited our favorite boutiques, enjoyed the best coffee, and treated ourselves to fresh pedicures. I confided in her about Phil sending me photos and subtle threats for months, and how much it messed with my head. The fallout with Phil made me fearful to trust my instincts.

It was over drinks at Lulu's that Chloe asked me what I'm going to do about Luca. "You're punishing yourself, Abbi. You love him."

"I love him," I admitted. "But can I trust him?"

"What do you think?" she challenged.

I shrug.

My best friend shook her head and in an eerily accurate impersonation of Gran, said, "Take a leap of faith, Abigail."

That was three hours ago. Now, I'm at the cemetery where I buried Gran nearly four months ago to the day. The days leading up to her funeral were chaotic. The planning and preparations kept me too busy to be inside my head. After I kissed her goodbye, I threw myself into job hunting, letting work consume me so I didn't have to think.

But right now, it's just me and the tombstones, and the full weight of losing Gran hits me. It's quickly followed by a pang of missing Luca. I wish he was here right now, slipping his hand in mine, meeting my Gran as I say the goodbye I've been holding back.

The thought surprises me and tears spring to my eyes. Jesus, I've cried more this week than in the past year and while I know on some level that I'm grieving, the display of emotion irks me.

Dry your eyes, lift your head, and straighten your spine.

Gran's voice floats through my mind as I slump next to her tombstone. It's a somber day in March, gray and cold and cloudy. It's fitting, given my mood, and I snuggle up against Gran's name, lovingly etched into the granite.

"I miss you, Gran," I sigh, tucking my knees up to my chest. I drag my fingers over the patches of grass, interspersed with hard ground and small rocks. The cemetery is empty today and I'm glad, since I have no idea how long I'll be sitting here, trying to find the words, the peace to move forward.

Are there any words to say goodbye to the person who means the most to you? Is there anything left to say, or do, once they're truly gone?

"I messed up," I force out. "Big time. But I guess you already knew that." During Gran's last months, I was spiraling from Phil. I spent as much time as possible with Gran and there were moments, snapshots, where she was lucid enough to recognize me. And every time a spark of awareness, a flicker of knowing, would spring into her eyes, she would remind me:

Dry your eyes, lift your head, and straighten your spine.

Even Gran knew I was devastated, beaten down by life. In those brief moments where I was me and she was still her, she saw me so clearly my chest ached.

Gran was not one to let life beat her down. She was fierce and brave and my rock.

A shaky sob escapes my throat as I clutch at a tuft of grass and rip it from the earth. "Why'd you leave me? You know I can't do this without you." My words are carried away with a gust of wind, scattered. I toss the blades of grass back down. "I met someone. A good man," I say, knowing in my heart that Luca is one of the best ones. "He may become a father," I add after a beat. "Do you think a man could be a good father and a good partner? Even if the two aren't connected?" I pause, turning to glance at Gran's name. *Ethel Walsh*. The sight of it causes me to smile.

"Anyway, I did what I always do. Ran. Hid." I sigh again, glancing up at the sky. Thick clouds are rolling in, angry and dark, filled with rain. "But how can I be with a guy who won't step up? Be a father to his kid?"

He doesn't know if it's his kid. In fact, he swears it isn't.

But wouldn't any guy do that? Not want the child?

The thought pops into my mind, quickly followed by shame. I think of Chloe's dad. I've never seen a man dote on his daughter the way Mr. C adores Chlo. I think of Noah and the way his face lights up when he reaches for Emmaline.

God, why am I so messed up? I tap the back of my head against Gran's tombstone and close my eyes. "Can I trust him, Gran?"

Silence meets my ears and then, a low rumble of thunder in the distance.

"Why do I keep chasing after the guys who lie and cheat? Why do I do stupid shit to impress them and pass up on the guys who are honest and sincere?"

The wind comes harder now, slapping against my cheeks. I lift my chin to meet it. A small smile curls the corners of my mouth because I can feel Gran's anger, her wrath. She hated when a woman spoke poorly of herself. She had no tolerance for self-pity either.

"Do you think he's the one?" I ask the emptiness. Except it's not empty because she's here. I can feel her in the hard ground beneath me, in the wicked wind around me, in the heavy sky above me. She's pressing in on me, fierce and bold and real.

"Tell me what to do!" I demand as the rain starts. It's only two or three drops before the entire sky opens and sheets pour down, thick and hard, pelting my skin like hail. Like pinches. I grin.

"I love you, Gran," I shout as lightning cracks the sky, unapologetically lighting up the city skyline. I laugh, shaking my head.

My gran was never the sweet, little old lady who knit scarves and baked cookies.

She was a tempest and always gave as good as she got. She raised me after all.

I revel in the storm, opening my palms to catch the rain, lifting my face to greet the wind. The breeze kisses my cheeks harshly and the thunder rolls through me like a hug, all encompassing.

"What do you think?" I whisper again, my eyes squeezed closed, my heart open to the signs she's gifting me.

Images of Luca flip through my mind on a loop. That first night, with his cocky smirk and smooth lines. Him, standing in goal, sure and confident and locked in. His dark, smoldering bedroom eyes, and the softness that rounds out his tone when he tells me he loves me. It's almost like I can feel his arms around me, phantom though they are, rooting me to this moment.

I've spent my life running from things that seem too good to be true. Maybe that's why I kept choosing the wrong men. Maybe deep down, I always knew I couldn't trust them and when they hurt me, it added to the self-fulfilling prophecy I kept feeding myself.

But Luca...his text messages, his defending me to his friends, his team, the whole damn world... Luca Pandatelli has proven over and over again that he'll show up for me. That I can trust him and count on him and need him.

Rain pelts my skin, sliding down my face. "What do you think, Gran?" I ask again, feeling my own resolve strengthen in my stomach. *Is he the one?*

Dry your eyes, lift your head, and straighten your spine.

The wind howls and thunder strikes.

My eyes pop open and I sit up, looking straight ahead as a figure, the most beautiful man I've ever laid eyes on, appears before me.

"What are you doing here, Luca?" I gasp, surprise rocking me harder than the thunder.

His blue eyes blaze, the hottest part of a flame, and his face smolders, an inferno. Luca's body is imposing on a normal day but right now, he's a giant, larger than life, and sent to me from her.

"I already told you; I'm all in, Abbi." His words, coupled with the sincerity of his expression, keep me pinned in place. Suddenly, I *know*. I accept what maybe I've known all along; Luca Pandatelli is worth taking a chance on. Not just a chance, but a risk. He's been chasing after my heart, my trust, for a while now and he's finally caught me. I *want* him to catch me.

"How'd you find me?" I push the wet clumps of hair away from my face, my hands slipping off my skin.

He steps toward me, his coat sopping wet, raindrops sliding down his face and dripping off his chin. But he doesn't drop his head, he doesn't do anything other than stare straight to my soul, to all the fear that dwells there.

"Did you really think I wouldn't come?"

I grin and his expression softens the slightest bit.

I hold my hands up and extend my arms. "Meet my Gran."

He chuckles as he sinks to his knees in front of me. "She makes one hell of an impression."

I nod in agreement.

"Just like her granddaughter," he adds softly and my heart bursts.

"I missed you," I admit, a lightness filling me up. Calm rolls through the emotional turmoil of moments ago, making me feel more secure and steady than I have in days.

"I love you," he says back. His big hand wraps around mine, folding it into a fist and holding on tight. "I'm not going anywhere without you."

"I want to be with you," I admit, knowing it's the truth on every level. "But if you're going to be a dad, I need you to be the best one," I blurt out.

His eyes crinkle as he smiles, a deep chuckle rumbling from his chest. Around us, the storm surges and softens, the sheets of rain petering out to a trickle as the clouds move east above our heads. "I'm not going to be a father. Yet."

"What do you mean?" I ask, my heart racing as Luca tightens his hold.

"I mean the real baby daddy came forward." He shifts closer, his face only inches from mine. "But one day, I want to have a whole hockey team of kids," he explains, his lips grazing mine. "Preferably with you." He kisses me, his mouth hot and demanding. The rain stops.

Thank you, Gran. I smile against his lips. "We'll see, Luca."

He chuckles, his hand cupping my cheek, his fingers brushing back my hair. "Hell yeah we will, Abbi."

I grip his wrist, keeping his hand anchored to my cheek. "I love you, Luca."

"I love you too, Abbi. And whatever this is"—he glances around the cemetery, before his eyes land on the skyline—"we'll work it all out together."

"Work what out?"

"Life," he says simply, kissing me again. I grow dizzy from it but when he pulls away, it's still too soon. "Come home with me?"

I nod. "My temporary suspension has been lifted. I'm back to work on Monday."

"That's great news, baby. But I didn't mean Boston."

My eyebrows lift, waiting.

"Philadelphia. Two weekends. My family is desperate to meet you. Claim you." He stands, pulling me up beside him.

"Claim me?"

He wraps an arm around my waist. "As one of ours. The Pandatellis are nothing if not possessive."

I giggle.

"And now that I've got you, Abbi"—he glances down at me, his face more serious than I've ever seen it—"there's not a chance in hell I'm letting you go."

I snuggle into his side. "We'll see."

He laughs and kisses the top of my head as we walk out of the cemetery. "This part is non-negotiable, love."

I smile and turn around for one last glance at Gran's tombstone. The sun is starting to shine again and the raindrops on the tombstone throw the light, glistening. Like a wink.

Take a leap of faith, Abigail.

So, I do.

CHAPTER 24
LUCA

"I swear, I'm good," Abbi says, cradling the phone between her shoulder and ear as she leans back on the couch in the hotel room I snagged. "Yes, I'm only two floors up from our room," she laughs, rolling her eyes. "I won't be mad if you head back to Boston, Chlo. In fact, I insist. Thanks for coming with me. Thanks for…everything. Yep," another chuckle. "Love you too."

She disconnects the call and I toss her a towel that she uses to dry her rain-soaked hair.

"Chloe's bouncing?" I ask, even though I've known all along that she would head out of town when I showed up.

"Yes, and you don't have to act surprised. I know she was your point of contact on all of this." Abbi gestures around the hotel room.

"Point of contact…" I scoff, moving over to the couch. "You're so professional."

She tosses her head back and laughs. "That's a lie and we both know it."

I grin but don't say anything else. I'm too focused on how her skin glistens as I peel her shirt off. Her breasts spring free and I work a swallow, all thoughts leaving my mind as my dick hardens. She smirks, knowing exactly what she's doing as she stands from the couch and relocates to the king-sized bed, wriggling out of her jeans on the way.

I follow closely behind, losing my hoodie, stepping out of my pants, and watching in anticipation as my girl leans back on the bed.

"Fancy," she murmurs, her eyes darting around the large hotel suite I booked on my train ride over.

I don't bother telling her that the hotel was nearly at capacity. I don't tell her anything because my throat is dry and my words have left me. She's rocking a dark green lingerie set, all lace, which surprises the hell out of me.

"Like this," I say, my index finger dragging over the edge of her bra. I watch in fascination as a trail of goosebumps flares over her skin in response. "Missed you, baby."

She sighs softly, her hands gripping my shoulders. Her nails dig in until I meet her eyes, acknowledge the apology there. "I'm sorry, Luca."

I shake my head. "Don't be. I should have—"

"You did everything right. I got scared." Her words are soft but I can see the confusion in her expression, hear the regret in her voice.

I dip forward, the space between us crackling with electricity. We're still coated in a spring rainstorm, our skin chilled, but suddenly, it feels like wildfire in my veins. Abbi's eyes blaze at whatever she reads in my expression, and I fight the urge to devour her whole.

"I love you, Abbi. I'm not going anywhere and I'm sure as hell not letting you walk away from me without an explanation. I know we have a lot to talk about and figure out. I know there's a lot of shit that needs to be explained, but right now—"

"Yes," she says simply.

"Yes, what?"

"Yes, I want you. Yes, I need you. And yes, I love you,

too," she replies, her fingertips fluttering over my skin, tracing my lower lip. "Make love to me, Luca. Please, make me yours."

Fireworks explode through my limbs, my heart rate jumping. I've never heard more beautiful words from a more beautiful woman. My hand cups her cheek, my thumb rough over her cheekbone as I close the space between us. When my lips touch hers, relief runs through me.

Abbi arches into my kiss, searching for my touch like she can't live without it. And right now, I can't consider a future that doesn't include her. I kiss her deeply, my tongue slipping into her mouth and dueling with hers. Our connection is needy. Desperate and powerful. Her fingers wrap around my wrist, both holding my hand to her face and squeezing enough to hurt.

We're blazing with emotion, fired up on old hurts and a need to erase them. I nip at her bottom lip and she whimpers, dropping her knees wider so I can settle more firmly in between them as my body shadows hers. My hands roam, memorizing the peaks and dips of her body, drunk on the smoothness of her skin.

I drag my mouth down the column of her neck as she yanks my hair, her legs encircling my hips.

"Need you, Luca," she pants.

"You have me, baby," I tell her, my words as serious as this moment, as hot as the friction flaring between us. I press my cock against her core and her eyes roll back in her head. "Not yet, Abs. I need more." I kiss the spot behind her ear and she bucks against me.

I drag her bra straps over her shoulders, pop the clasp, and watch as it falls away. Then, I drag her panties over her hips, my entire being short-circuiting when she's laid out before me, naked and perfect and staring at me with more trust than vulnerability. She's completely bare, body and heart, and I revel in her trust.

"I won't ever hurt you," I tell her, staring into her eyes as I kick off my boxers. "I won't ever lie or cheat or give you a reason to doubt me."

Her lips part and her eyes widen. She studies me and the space surrounding us shrinks, causing this moment to hold more weight, more significance, than any before it. This, right now, is the turning point. We're either all in or we're not. And I want to be one-hundred percent in with Abbi.

"I won't ever run from you," she says finally, her voice cracking. Her eyes bore into mine, her fingers curling around the bedsheets. "Or hide. Or give you a reason to doubt me."

Her words cause the last bit of my restraint to slip and I'm on her, kissing her with everything I can't express. Not because I'm scared but because there aren't words to convey how deeply I feel for her. Want her. Cherish her.

I kiss every inch of her skin, nipping and tasting. She tracks every muscle in my back and arms, feeling and squeezing. When my tongue parts her core, she bucks off the bed, the sweetest moan I've ever heard falling from her lips. Our frantic and fierce gives way to sweet and gentle as I love her with my mouth, with my hands, with everything I have to offer.

Before Abbi shatters, I rock into her, gathering her against my chest. Her hair is damp as I kiss her temple, murmuring sweet nothings as she clings to me. We make love slowly, relishing the moment, savoring each other. And we finally crest and break, I'm drowning in her eyes and she's whispering my name.

"THIS IS where I puked on my twenty-first birthday." Abbi

points to a curb in a parking lot as we pass, on our way to dinner.

"You're really giving me the scenic tour, aren't you?" I joke, ruffling her hair.

She shoots me a grin. "Boston is the first new place I ever lived," she says, but her words hold a gravity that causes me to falter.

"Wait." I stop walking and touch her wrist until she stills beside me. "You were born here? In Hoboken?"

She nods, a smile flitting over her lips. "For a long time, I thought I was staying for Gran. It wasn't until I was in Boston and things seemed…hard, that I realized maybe I stayed for me too. Because it was safe. Familiar." She shrugs. "But I just wanted to come back, see Gran, and then leave on my own terms. Knowingly take a step forward that seemed hopeful, and not like I was running away."

"I get that," I tell her truthfully, my fingers wrapping around her elbow. I pull her into my side and plant a kiss on the crown of her head. "I'm proud of you, Abbi."

"Don't be."

I pull back and gaze down at her. "But I am." I pull open the door to the restaurant, a Cuban place she swore has the best skirt steak and plantains. "Always," I add as she slips in front of me.

She turns back to smile and in it, I see my forever. I'm so lost in the look on Abbi's expression that she literally slams into a man, pulling us both up short.

Except when I look up, my hands on Abbi's waist to steady her, anger replaces my good time vibes.

"Phil," Abbi breathes out, her voice shaky. Immediately, her limbs lock down and she stands ramrod straight, the bones of her hips jutting into my palms.

"Abbi," he murmurs, his jaw slack and his eyes wide. Guess he wasn't expecting to run into her after he ran her out of town.

I freeze, waiting to take my cue from Abbi even though I want to cock my fist back and let it fly at Phil's face for causing my girl so much goddamn heartache.

"Abbi," a female voice echoes as a woman appears at Phil's side, her belly huge.

"Melanie," Abbi says curtly. She shuffles back the slightest bit but in that movement, everything shifts. Her back grazes my chest, her hands find mine, and I puff out like a damn peacock because my girl is leaning into me and I literally got her back.

"How's it going?" I ask, flashing a saccharine smile.

Phil's gaze narrows as he glares at me while Melanie's face lights up, a relief that would be pathetic if it wasn't so potent, coloring her eyes. Damn, Phil Rickens is a fucking jackass.

"Pa-Panda," Phil stutters, his eyes flashing down to Abbi.

"Good to see you again," I manage to keep my voice even.

"You're in Hoboken now?" he asks but I know what he's really asking: did I relocate here?

"Abbi's just showing me around," I give a non-answer and shuffle Abbi and me to the side so Phil and his wife can pass.

"The Ropa Vieja is wonderful," Melanie says and I feel sorry for her and the child she's carrying. Because while she hasn't slipped her hand away from Phil's arm, he hasn't bothered to look at her once.

Instead, his gaze burns through Abbi and my anger jumps several notches. Still, I wait on Abbi, knowing that she needs to conclude this moment, to find some slice of closure in it. And fuck, that pisses me off.

"It is," Abbi murmurs, her gaze darting to Melanie. "The next time you come, after you deliver, you should try their twist on the mojito. It's amazing."

Melanie's free hand covers her belly and she shoots Abbi a grateful smile. I have no clue what the hell is transpiring between them but it's something because Abbi relaxes the tiniest bit and Melanie's expression softens.

"It's a boy," Melanie says.

"Congratulations, to you both," Abbi replies, her gaze trained on Melanie.

"So, you moved here?" Phil asks, so fucking obvious that I have to bite back my laughter.

"No, Phil," Abbi answers, her voice hardening as her gaze snaps to his. "I relocated to Boston. Permanently. And I'm not leaving, even though you did your damnedest by leaking those photos."

Melanie inhales sharply and Phil pales.

But my girl tips her head back and smiles up at me. "I got too comfortable there," she adds.

Phil blanches and I dip my eyebrows together, but Abbi shakes her head.

"You moved for Panda?" Phil's voice holds an edge I dislike even more than him fucking questioning her like he has any right to information about Abbi's life and how she's living it.

"I moved for a job," she says evenly. She squeezes my hand and I squeeze back. Abbi turns and flashes me a grateful smile. "Luca and I reconnected there."

"Reconnected?" Phil repeats as Melanie shuffles uncomfortably beside him.

"Yeah," I say, never taking my eyes off Abbi. "I couldn't just give up on my forever."

Abbi looks startled for one heartbeat before she beams, her smile radiant and just for me. I grin back and it's as if the entire restaurant falls away.

Phil clearing his throat brings me back to the present and I shoot him an irritated look. "Good luck, man, with everything," I say, surprised that I mean it when I take in Melanie again. Good thing she seems to be genuine, for the kid's sake.

"Have a good night," Melanie replies civilly as she ushers her husband through the doors.

A cold blast shoots through the entryway until the door closes and it's just Abbi and me.

My girl hasn't stopped smiling. "Your forever, huh?"

I chuckle and tap her ass.

"You mean it?" she asks playfully, her eyes still on mine.

"Every word, Abbi."

She turns into me and kisses me hard as a whistle and applause ring out behind her. When she pulls away, her cheeks flushing, I smirk at the hostess fanning herself with a menu.

"I feel like I've waited my whole life to see that," the hostess laughs.

Abbi squeals and throws her arms around the girl. "Veronica! I miss you!"

Veronica laughs and pats Abbi's back. "Me too. I'd say welcome home but..." She trails off as she glances at me.

"But I'm already home," Abbi finishes, turning to smile at me once more.

"He's a lot prettier than Hoboken," Veronica supplies and we all laugh.

Veronica seats us at a corner table and Abbi orders us a round of mojitos. A candle flickers between us, casting her face in a soft glow. But her eyes blaze, more alive than I've ever seen them. The knowledge that I put that heat there, that I eased some of her fears, that she's finding the closure from her past that she needs, allows me to relax in my chair and enjoy this moment with my girl.

"Welcome to Hoboken, Luca," Abbi says when our drinks arrive, lifting a mojito in my direction.

I tap my glass against hers. "Welcome home, baby," I reply, widening my eyes and gesturing toward myself.

She laughs and shakes her head. "We'll see," she says but I

hear the promise in her voice. And I see my whole future in her eyes.

CHAPTER 25
ABBI

"What if they don't like me?" I whisper frantically as we turn the corner onto Luca's street.

"They're going to love you," he replies easily, like we're going to grab a coffee and he's not about to throw me to the wolves.

Not that his family are wolves, it's more that I feel hopped up on nerves and adrenaline about meeting people I desperately want to impress, even knowing that they've all most likely seen me naked. *Those damn photos.*

"Yeah, what's not to love," I mutter, my tone dripping with sarcasm.

"Exactly," my man says cheerfully.

I shoot him a look and he chuckles. He stops a few houses away from his father's and plants his hands on my hips, steadying me. "Baby, look at me."

I do and at the easy smile on his lips, I fight the urge to kiss him. It's been two weeks since Luca brought me home from Hoboken and I've spent every night wrapped up in his arms, wondering how the hell I got so lucky.

"My family is dying to meet you. They have been since the

moment my nieces and nephews told them about FaceTiming with you."

I laugh.

"They've been rooting for you since the beginning because they know, as does everyone, that you make me so goddamn happy. Don't worry about anything except enjoying yourself. Because while my family is loud and nosy and doesn't understand a thing about personal space, they're also loving and empathetic and will do everything they can to make you feel comfortable."

I breathe out a shaky breath and nod. "You swear?"

"Promise it, Abs." He places his hands on the sides of my face and looks into my eyes for a long beat. In their blue depths, I see the truth of his words and I lean into that, into him, as I lift my chin and he lowers his mouth. He kisses me deeply until I pull back. Then, he smacks my ass and gets me moving in the right direction again.

"I saw that!" a little kid shouts from a front porch and I cringe as Luca's laughter rings out.

"You're a little shit, Jack!" he hollers at his nephew.

"Uncle Luca's kissing his girlfriend," the boy yells into the open door and I hear the flurry of excitement before a swell of people push out onto the porch, completely unconcerned about the cold, damp weather.

Luca groans as I laugh.

"Don't embarrass him, Jack," a woman scolds.

"Ooh, she's beautiful," another woman comments.

"Gino, put a coat on," a man bellows.

"Close the door!" someone hollers.

"Come in and get warm!" Another woman waves at us.

"Welcome to the crazy," Luca murmurs in my ear but I hear the happiness in his voice.

I grin at his family, huddled on the porch, as we draw closer. "Hi!" I wave. "I'm Abbi."

"Oh darling, we know who you are," one of the women, I think Luca's sister-in-law Nella says, and my stomach sinks.

"You're the only woman who's managed to wrangle my brother," the other woman responds easily.

"And we want to know exactly how you did it," the first woman laughs.

Luca swears as a bubble of laughter swells in my throat. "We're going to need drinks for that," I joke.

"Wine or vodka?" The man, Luca's brother by the strong resemblance, pokes his head out the door.

"Bring both." The third woman, Justine who I met on FaceTime, shoos him back inside.

This time, I do laugh. "It's nice to meet you all." I take the first step and am pulled into warm embraces.

"Girl, you have no idea," Luca's sister says.

"STOP!" I throw up my hand as Luca's sister Justine shares an incredibly embarrassing story about a three-year-old Luca catching his penis in his zipper his first day of preschool. I'm laughing so hard, I can't breathe. "That's awful."

"What's awful is you guys telling Abbi this," Luca scolds them but amusement colors his expression.

"Please." Justine flicks her wrist. "She never would have made it this far if she wasn't cut out for the real stories."

"Real stories," Luca scoffs.

"You guys are hilarious. Holidays at your house must have been so fun growing up," I say, glancing around the group.

We're packed into Luca's father's living room and while the room is bursting at the seams, it's all warmth and love and family. I'm reveling in it, soaking up each moment like a cultural experience. I've never met a family like the Pandatellis before. They finish each other's thoughts, have several conversations going at once that everyone is somehow engaged in, and don't miss any of the little pranks the kids try to pull off.

Overall, I'm incredibly impressed and want to spend the rest of the weekend wrapped up in their infectious energy.

"It was the best," Justine says softly, her eyes taking on a faraway glow. "We always put the tree there." She points to a corner of the room.

"It never fits," Luca's brother Robbie explains, topping up my wine glass. "And some of the ornaments always break."

"Remember Gino's first Christmas when we unwrapped the stockings—" Nikki starts.

"And it said 'Gina,'" Jack finishes, cackling.

Gino shoots him a sour look.

"Pop dresses up as Santa," Laura whispers to me. "He thinks we don't know it's him but…" Her voice trails off as she gives me a knowing look, her gaze darting between Luca's father and me.

I stifle my laughter and tip my head in understanding. No disguise in the world could conceal the sharpness in Mr. Pandatelli's electric blue eyes.

While the rest of the family embraced me with open arms and a never-ending list of questions, Mr. Pandatelli hasn't said much beyond a greeting. But I've felt his gaze on me for most of the evening, studying my reactions, listening to my words. He's the only Pandatelli I can't get a read on and it makes me nervous, since his stamp of approval seems the most important.

But when I glance at Luca, he's as laid-back as ever. An easy grin coats his lips and his eyes dance with laughter at the shenanigans his nieces and nephews concoct.

"We're all going to Luca's game the second weekend in April. I think it's the twelfth," Nikki says. "You should come with us."

Mentally, I pull up Luca's game schedule. "Oh, they're in Philadelphia that weekend."

"Yeah," Justine laughs.

"I'd love to," I say, happy to be included in anything this family does.

"I'm going to heat up the sauce and meatballs. Start boiling the water for ravioli." Jenni, Luca's sweet stepmother, stands.

"I'll help you," Nikki offers.

"Me too." Nella shoots to her feet.

"Come on, gang. Let's go get cleaned up for supper." Justine rises, gesturing to the cohort of cousins.

"Hey, Luca, I wanted to ask you about this sound my car's been making," Robbie says, gesturing toward the front door. "Mind taking a walk?"

Luca breathes out a sigh and gets to his feet. "You good?" he asks me.

I feel the weight of Mr. Pandatelli's gaze. "I'm great," I reply easily, my eyes closing as Luca brushes a kiss over my forehead.

Silence sweeps the living room and I know that this, leaving me with Luca's father, is intentional. The front door closes.

"They're subtle, my family," Mr. Pandatelli says, his voice gravelly.

I laugh lightly, trying to relax in my chair.

Straighten your spine.

I shoot ramrod straight again, perched on the edge of my seat. "It's nice to finally meet you, Mr. Pandatelli."

He dips his head in acknowledgement.

A flurry of nerves skates up my arms. I'm way out of my

wheelhouse here. Having never had a father figure in my life, I don't know the protocol for this kind of conversation.

"How did you meet my son?" he asks finally, swirling his wine.

"At a bar," I answer honestly, meeting his gaze. I have no clue what Luca's father hopes to achieve from our chat, but I do know that he'll pick up on any fib I try to feed him. "It was over the summer. I was at a bachelorette party."

"You both were drinking?"

"Yes."

He takes a sip of his wine. "And then?"

"And then, I went back to Hoboken and—"

"And I had a heart attack," he surmises.

I clear my throat and nod.

Suddenly, his expression clears and a smile, so much like Luca's, crosses his face. I inhale sharply as time plays a trick on me, offering a glimpse of the man Luca will grow into decades from now. "So, you and my son have been…interested in each other for nearly a year."

"Yes," I agree, my eyebrows pulling together. Has it really been almost a year since Luca and I met? And how much has changed in such a short amount of time…

"It's been a hard year for you," Mr. Pandatelli states.

"Yes."

"And for Luca," he adds.

I look up, meeting his gaze.

"My son has shouldered a lot of responsibility for this family for a long time. Too long." Some of Luca's words from the night we met, some of his actions as I've gotten to know him, flicker through my mind. "I relied on him a little too much."

I bite my lip, unsure of what to say.

Luckily, Mr. Pandatelli continues. "He's a good man. One who needs to start taking more time for himself, more time to build his future. You're the first woman he's ever brought home. And you'll be the last."

I gasp, his words shocking me.

"They like you, all of them." He lifts his chin toward the kitchen where female laughter rings out.

"And you?" I ask, my nerves hijacking my body. For some reason, his response matters the most.

He pauses, his eyes boring into mine. "Do you like scotch, Abbi?" he asks after a moment.

"I do."

Mr. Pandatelli smiles, his eyes warm. "Can you pour us some?" He flicks his wrist to the bar that sits in the corner of the room.

I stand on shaky legs and cross the room, wondering what kind of test this is and even more importantly, how the hell I'm faring? I pick up a bottle of scotch but Mr. Pandatelli tsks.

"Not that one. The Macallan. Inside the bar," he says. "Three fingers."

I follow his directions and pour us each a glass. When I pass him a tumbler, he places his fingers over mine and holds, his eyes warm. "Thank you for bringing back my son, Abbi."

Tears spring to my eyes as I understand the meaning behind his words. Just like Luca's love healed the broken parts of me, I've done the same for him.

"I love your son, Mr. Pandatelli."

"I know. He's head over heels for you, too," he replies, releasing his hold and clinking his glass against mine. He lifts the glass to his lips as I sink into the chair beside him. "And I couldn't be prouder," he murmurs before taking a drink.

Relief courses through me as I sip the strong scotch, letting its heat settle my nerves.

In the next moment, Luca and Robbie reenter the living room, their conversation halting as they take Mr. Pandatelli and me in, sitting here, drinking Macallan.

Robbie clasps his brother on the back and Luca beams, giving me a look of pure love, mixed with a thread of heat.

"Robbie," Mr. Pandatelli calls his son over.

But I can't tear my eyes away from Luca.

"I love you," he mouths to me.

"I love you more," I murmur.

Then, we're called to supper and I lose myself in the rambunctious, loud, loving energy of the Pandatelli family, knowing in my heart of hearts that I am finally home.

CHAPTER 26
LUCA

I grin up at the stands, seeing Abbi sandwiched in between Justine and Nikki, Valentina on her lap.

"Man, your family is a trip," Austin says to me, shaking his head as my nieces and nephews begin to dance.

"They're a social liability," I respond, but the warmth in my tone takes the sting out of my words.

Noah laughs. "They can give the Merricks a run for their money."

Austin chuckles. "That's the truth." He clasps me on the shoulder. "I'm happy for you, Panda."

My gaze latches onto Abbi, her eyes finding mine even through the thousands of people here tonight. She blows me a kiss and my smile widens. "Me too," I tell Cap.

"Austin, we've got a problem." Sims rushes up to us.

"What's wrong?" Austin asks.

The team huddles around Sims.

"It's Yaeger. He's gone," Sims explains.

"Gone? What the hell do you mean, gone?" Easton snaps.

Sims shrugs. "He was in the locker room, suiting up, when his phone rang."

"He took the call outside," Evans supplies.

"And never came back in," Sims says.

"His car is gone but his watch, his bag, everything is still in his locker," Evans adds.

Austin swears, scraping a hand over his face.

"It must have been some kind of emergency," I say, doing damage control. It's Yaeger's first season starting with the Hawks, and he's a solid player, an all-around good guy. "The only way he would up and leave is—"

"If something devastating happened," Noah agrees.

"He's not answering his phone," Sims confirms.

"Okay, we've gotta focus on the game," Austin says, his gaze swinging to Coach Phillips.

By the tightness in his expression, he's already been informed of the situation. "Keller! You're up!" Coach shouts at one of the newer guys on the team who looks truly petrified about being tossed into his first NHL game.

The guys and I exchange a look, all of us recalling our first games, the fear and the nerves and the uncertainty of it all. Then we rally around Keller, hyping him up for the first game of his career.

True terror flickers in his expression as he looks at me, his eyes blown with panic.

"Look, you're going to go out there and mess up," I tell him.

"Jesus, Panda." Noah smacks the back of my head.

"And after the first mistake, you're gonna settle in," I coach Keller. "We've all been where you are, dude, and we've all made mistakes. But after you get that out of your system, you'll be fine. You've been training your entire life for this moment—"

Keller's face pales.

East swears.

I grin. "Keller"—I grip his shoulder and give it a little shake, switching tactics—"you're gonna be a goddamn rock star. Now go out there and let's win this game!" I release him and he stumbles toward the ice.

"Don't ever go into motivational speaking," Noah advises me as he pushes off behind Keller.

"He'll be fine," I say, watching Keller.

"After he makes his first fuckup," East agrees and we share a laugh.

"I hope Yaeger's all right," I say.

East nods. "It must have been some emergency…"

"Must have been a woman," I surmise, my gaze finding Abbi again.

"Yep," East agrees, his attention snagged by Claire.

"You guys are fucking pussy whipped," Sims says, his voice laced with disgust.

"You'll see," I tell Sims over my shoulder as I skate onto the ice. "One day, it'll happen to you."

"No way," he swears.

Easton chuckles.

But once I'm on the ice, I block everything out and zone in on the game. Hockey has been the one constant in my life, the only thing besides my family that I had before my mom passed and afterwards. But now my family includes Abbi Walsh, and I know that everything is different. For the better.

I fell in love for the first time in my life with the most incredible woman I've ever known. For the first time ever, I allow myself to hope. And it feels even better than saving a buzzer-beater goal and winning a game in my hometown with my family cheering in the stands.

"THAT WAS ONE HELL OF A SAVE," Abbi murmurs as I kiss her hard after the game.

"Great game, bro!" Nikki hits me on the back.

"You were amazing!" Justine gushes, squeezing me in a hug.

"That was awesome!" Jack hollers as Gino rushes my legs, nearly toppling me over.

I shoot Abbi an apologetic look as I'm pulled away from her by my rowdy nephews.

But her face is shining, her eyes are warm, and she looks truly happy.

Pop pulls her into a conversation, and I watch in awe as the man known for being the strong, but silent, type chatters away like a schoolgirl.

Abbi has that effect on people. She's impossible not to fall in love with.

I would know; she had me from that first night. And I haven't looked back once.

EPILOGUE

ABBI

Two Years Later

I pace back and forth in front of the bathroom sink, too nervous to look at the pregnancy test. My engagement ring throws the sunlight and I grin, twisting the wedding band around my finger. Luca and I married last summer in Philadelphia. It was a small wedding but loud as hell as the Pandatellis know how to party. Between Luca's family, the Crawfords, and the team, we were surrounded by love and genuine well-wishers.

I glance at my phone, excitement and nerves squeezing the pit of my stomach. One more minute until I can look. Oh, how desperately I want to be pregnant. Luca and I haven't been trying that long, only three months, and still, waiting each month is agony.

My phone dings and I peek at the screen. Twenty seconds to go.

LUCA

Bringing home Mexican for dinner. Make margaritas.

I grin. I really hope we won't be drinking margaritas but still have something to celebrate.

I take a deep breath, knowing it's time to look at the test. A wave of nerves buzzes through me. I squeeze my eyes shut tight.

Whatever the test says, it's fine. Everything is good.

Take a leap of faith, Abigail.

I let out a shaky exhale and lean over the vanity.

Two pink lines greet me and I squeal, throwing my arms in the air. Oh my God, I'm pregnant! Luca and I are going to have a baby. A baby!

My phone beeps and I grin, picking it up.

LUCA

On my way home.

His message spurs me into action. I quickly tuck the pregnancy test in the vanity drawer. Assessing my reflection, I fluff my hair and apply some perfume and lipstick. I hurry into the bedroom to retrieve the present I purchased the month after my wedding, hoping beyond hope that one day, I'd be able to give it to Luca.

I tuck the gift bag out of sight and set the kitchen table. I'm just filling the water glasses when I hear the front door open.

"Honey, I'm home!" Luca announces.

"In the kitchen."

He enters the room and my breath lodges in my throat. Will I ever not have this reaction to him? Will he always make my heart race? Can I love him any more than I do right now?

"Hi, baby," he murmurs, dropping a kiss to my lips. "Hungry?"

I nod, too excited to speak. Do I tell him now? After we eat? Tonight?

"Okay," he says, placing the takeout bag on the table and unpacking our dinner.

I shuffle from one foot to the other.

"Abbi?" Luca turns, frowning. "You okay?"

I nod, grinning so hard my cheeks ache.

Luca chuckles, tilting his head as he studies me. "What's going on? Want a margarita?" He glances around, probably wondering where the tequila is.

"We're having a baby!" I announce, unable to keep my secret for a moment longer.

Since I'm staring straight at him, I have the privilege of witnessing the sheer joy that ripples across Luca's face. His eyes widen, a blue brighter than a summer sky. His lips part, disbelief curling the corners upward. And pure wonder colors his gaze, filling me up with more love than I've ever known. "We are?"

I nod, tears springing to my eyes. I laugh and lift my hand, wicking away a tear. "It's the hormones."

"It is?" He moves closer, his hands settling on my hips. "We're pregnant," he whispers, kissing me.

"We're pregnant," I murmur. "Oh, I almost forgot." I scurry away to grab the gift bag. I pass it to him.

Luca grins at me as he reaches into the bag and pulls out the sweetest Hawks onesie. "Oh God," he laughs. "I love it." His eyes find mine again. "I can't believe this."

"I know!"

"When did you find out? Are you hungry? Thirsty? Tired?" he asks, his hands finding my hips again.

"Happy," I tell him truthfully.

"Me too. So fucking happy. I love you, Abbi." He kisses me softly, one of his hands caressing my stomach. "And I love you too," he says, looking down at my abdomen.

My heart turns to mush at that and I wrap my arms

around Luca's shoulders, pulling him close and kissing him hard.

He moans into my mouth. "You hungry, baby?"

"Uh-huh," I say, dragging my mouth down the side of his neck. "But not for food."

Luca chuckles, lifting me gently in his arms and walking us toward our bedroom. "I already love this pregnancy thing."

"It's the hormones," I joke, as he places me in the center of our bed.

Luca steps back and studies me. He bites his lower lip and pulls his shirt over his head, discarding it on the floor. My eyes widen and Luca chuckles. "Yeah, okay. We'll see, baby."

I laugh as he moves up my body. Luca kisses me passionately and I lose myself in his touch as he reminds me just how good we are at making babies.

A whole hockey team.

THANK you so much for reading *The Heart Chaser*! I hope you loved Abbi and Luca's story.

ARE you wondering where Yaeger disappeared to? If second chance, homecoming, marriage of convenience romances are your jam, dive into The Trailblazer!

THE TRAILBLAZER

CHAPTER ONE - DECLAN

The arena pulses with energy, an infectious excitement and enthusiasm for tonight's game that carries into the locker room.

It washes over me, demanding that I mentally lock in. It hypes me up, reminding me how fortunate I am. How many people turn their childhood dream into reality? How many little kids with a pair of skates and a hockey stick dream of playing in the NHL?

It's my first season starting for the Boston Hawks and each time I take the ice, gratitude for my stubbornness, persistence, and the luck of the Irish, mainly in the form of Beau Harrison, the man who paved my way for a hockey career, rolls through me. I take a deep breath and try to calm my nerves. I toss up a prayer and move to close my locker door when my phone buzzes with an incoming call.

As soon as Da's name flashes across the screen, a ball of dread forms in the pit of my stomach. Something's happened. There's no way Da would call right before a game, a game he's most likely tuning into, unless something is wrong.

"Da, what's wrong?" I answer immediately.

He sighs. "I'm sorry, Declan. Mr. Harrison passed."

His words slam into me with the strength of a slap shot: hard, quick, and devastating. I gesture to a guy on my team that I'm stepping out to talk to Da. Once in the hallway, I sink down onto a bench, gripping the phone until my knuckles pop.

"When?" I whisper, my tone raw with emotion.

"Four days ago."

"Four days? When's the funeral?" A note of panic laces my tone. Did I miss it? Miss saying goodbye to the man who shaped my future?

"The family had a small, private ceremony. He was cremated. I'm sorry, son. I know how much he meant to you." Da sighs, "There aren't many men like Beau left in the world."

How's Vivi? I'm desperate to ask but years of silence between me and the girl who once owned my heart causes me to hold my tongue. Instead, I work a swallow, guilt expanding through my chest. "I just spoke to him two, maybe three weeks ago. He asked me to send some signed hockey gear for one of the youth camps his foundation runs. He was so...proud."

"He was always proud of you," Da agrees. Da worked as the head grounds caretaker on Beau Harrison's estate my entire childhood. It wasn't until I started university that Da moved back to his native Ireland. At that point, Mr. Harrison's granddaughter Vivi and I had broken up and without Da or Vivi to visit in Tennessee, Mr. Harrison became my only point of contact in the place that raised me. And now, he's gone... "How did he die?"

"A heart attack. He's been having trouble for quite some time. He just kept it quiet. I only heard occasional updates from Mrs. Stevens," Da explains, referencing another employee of Mr. Harrison's. "Genevieve's taking it hard."

Vivi. My heart twists thinking of her. How is she handling the news? Is she alone, walking the halls of the mansion she was raised in? Or maybe in a downtown bar, drinking to her granddaddy's legacy with a group of friends. I frown, realizing I know nothing about her life now. I know nothing about her.

But the last time I spoke to Mr. Harrison… "He asked me to look out for her. When I spoke to him, he asked me, and I laughed it off. He knew…" I trail off again, trying to make sense of the news. "I haven't spoken to Vivi in seven years." But I've never stopped thinking of Genevieve Rae, my Vivi. She was the one that got away, the one I never got over. Even though I clung to my relationship with her granddaddy all these years, we never spoke of Vivi. Not until that last conversation…

"Well, if you don't get to Nashville by tomorrow, you won't be able to honor that request." Da's brogue is thicker, filled with emotion and the pain of losing his old friend.

"What are you talking about?" I demand.

"She's getting married."

Those three words stop me short. They pull something in my chest, something I locked away years ago, until it unravels, unravelling me.

"To whom?" I whisper, a new type of fear skating up my arms. There's no way Vivi wouldn't postpone her wedding in the wake of her granddaddy's death. Mr. Harrison was more like a father to Vivi anyway. Her mom died in childbirth and her dad is a career military officer, usually deployed. Vivi wouldn't celebrate anything, much less a wedding, five goddamn days after Mr. Harrison's passing. Something is off; it doesn't *feel* right. "This doesn't make any sense."

"Henry Stevens," Da offers, naming Mrs. Stevens' son, one of my childhood buddies. Henry, Vivi, and I grew up together on the Harrison Estate.

Memories of long forgotten days roll through my mind with sharp precision. Henry, Genevieve, and me swinging from a rope into the creek, climbing trees, racing each other to the top, bike riding around town, and eating ice cream cones on Saturday afternoons. While Vivi and Henry were close, we always knew, all three of us, that Vivi and I were forever. That our connection outpaced any childhood friendship or adolescent puppy love.

At least, I thought we did. Until Vivi and I broke up the summer before college, I went to Ireland with Da, and she stopped returning my calls. Instead of the friendship we promised each other, Vivi stomped all over my heart, and we moved down two different paths with two very different endings.

Genevieve Rae is marrying Henry Stevens.

The words don't compute in my brain because they're all fucking wrong. She can't marry him. She can't marry…

But can't she? An old memory, one I worked hard to forget, flairs to life in my mind. The one time I returned to Tennessee after leaving for the University of Minnesota. It was my sophomore year of college and I had to see her; I had to know why she cut me off the way she did. When I hugged her goodbye before my trip, we swore we'd still talk, that we'd be in each other's lives no matter what. I tried. Why didn't she?

When I saw her with Henry, I knew. They were laughing, messing around with boxing gloves behind the small house Henry's family occupied. He was training her but his hands, they touched her with familiarity, with confidence. The blustering friend of my childhood had grown into a man who knew my girl better than I did.

Unable to stomach it, I left. I haven't seen her since.

The cheers from the arena reverberate down the hallway, capturing my attention again.

"Da, I appreciate you calling but I'm about to skate out on—"

"Hockey isn't everything, son." Da's voice holds an edge, something I don't fully understand.

"We broke up," I remind him. "We haven't talked in years."

"Have you not thought of her in that long too?"

I swear, because Da knows damn well that not a day passes without my thinking of Genevieve. About the promises we made and the future we dreamed up. About the friendship we swore meant everything, no matter where we went to college, no matter what happened afterwards.

But then I left for Minnesota and she…fell in love with Henry fucking Stevens. I saw it with my own eyes the following year.

"It's not too late," Da murmurs. "You've still got time, son."

"Time for what?" I scoff, frustrated and angry and so fucking gutted by the news Da shared. Mr. Harrison is dead. Vivi's getting married. The arena is waiting. My head spins, my emotions pulled in too many conflicting directions.

"To get your girl."

"Right," I say sarcastically. "I gotta go, Da." I hang up.

But I don't stand from the bench. Instead, I fist my phone and feel the gut-wrenching sadness of Mr. Harrison's loss mix with the terrifying realization that I can't lose Vivi. Not forever, not without knowing what went wrong, not without…telling her that I never truly moved on.

Before I can overthink it, I pull off my jersey and re-enter the silent locker room. I change into sweats. I rush down the hallway of The Meadows, away from the arena, toward the parking lot and my waiting SUV. I blow off a NHL hockey game as a defenseman for the Boston Hawks, the career opportunity of a lifetime, to drive seventeen hours to break up a wedding. But not any wedding. Vivi's.

I lost my fucking mind.

It's the only thing that makes sense as the high of adrenaline, the wave of fear, I've been riding for nearly seventeen hours on my drive home to Tennessee morphs into fatigue.

I take the turn toward my tiny hometown, on the outskirts of Nashville. My parents moved here when I was a kid, my father's family unhappy that he fell for an American instead of an Irishwoman. It was hypocritical bullshit if you ask me since my father's mother married a German. But we don't talk about my grandfather, the guy who hit it and quit it, leaving nothing behind but his last name and a dark stain on my family's reputation in a small, Irish village.

After mom passed when I was five, Da stayed in Tennessee, happily employed by Mr. Harrison. It wasn't until I accepted a hockey scholarship to the University of Minnesota that Da agreed to move back to his homeland.

While my whole family now resides in Ireland, the one I made as a child in Tennessee still claims a piece of my soul. Genevieve Rae still holds a piece of my heart.

Which is why, after seventeen long hours, I enter the small town we both call home, and scan every passerby for her wild, blonde waves and bright, sky blue eyes.

Driving down Main Street, my life in Boston falls away. Instead, I see a million memories from before Boston and the NHL, from before hockey. I see Vivi eating strawberry ice cream cones with chocolate sprinkles. Mrs. Grant in her green apron, waving us past her shop on our bicycles, after stuffing our pockets with candy. I see the old public library where Vivi taught me how to read and the corner store where I bought her a bracelet for her twelfth birthday. That was the first time she kissed me, and I don't know if I ever truly came up for oxygen since. Because when my lips touched hers, everything I thought I knew disappeared and everything I thought I wanted changed.

I wanted her.

Shaking my head, I turn off Main Street toward a bed-and-breakfast Da told me Mrs. Cleary still runs in the heart of the historic district. I park my SUV and grab the small bag I keep in the back for emergencies—usually of the hockey variety—but right now, I'm glad it's stocked with two changes of clothes, clean underwear, and a toothbrush. It also holds a couple hundred-dollar bills and my passport, which is a relief, since I left my wallet in my locker at The Meadows. Shouldering my bag, I make my way inside.

Mrs. Cleary turns and smiles when the bell alerts her to my arrival but when she spots me her mouth drops open and tears spring to the corners of her eyes.

"Declan Yaeger, my word, is that really you?" she asks, her hands gripping the skirt of her dress.

I smile, knowing the moment my dimple pops because Mrs. Cleary's expression softens. "It's me, Mrs. C."

"Oh, welcome home," she sighs, hurrying around the counter and wrapping me up in a big hug that feels the same as it did when I was nine and flipped over the handlebars of my bike out front.

I breathe in the cinnamon and sugar that clings to her, years of making scones before the rest of town is awake, and feel a strange sensation move through my chest. The world suddenly shifts, straightens, and a wave of homesickness, a longing for what was, crashes over me.

Mrs. Cleary grips my shoulders and pulls back, offering a hopeful smile. "You're here for her, aren't you?"

I nod, my brow furrowing. "How'd you know?"

She laughs lightly. "Genevieve has that effect."

I smile. She sure does.

"Besides, we haven't seen you here in years."

Her words cause guilt to swell inside but I bite the corner of my mouth and nod in acknowledgement. There's no way I'm going to admit that the one time I did come home, my heart splintered all over again. After that, it never made sense. Why would I come back here if I wasn't coming home to Genevieve?

But right now, staring at Mrs. Cleary, noting the gray strands running through her hair, the wrinkles bracketing her mouth, I feel ashamed for staying away so long.

"We're all really proud of you, Declan," she says, making me feel worse.

"Thank you," I say quietly, undeserving of her praise. I never would have made it as far as I did without the support of Mr. Harrison. His commitment to me, to hockey, created my future. Him and Vivi and Da. This town. "Does she love him?" I dip my head, unsure if I want the answer.

She must, right? Genevieve Rae wouldn't marry for anything less than love. But how could anything be greater than what we once had?

Mrs. Cleary grips my hand and squeezes until I meet her eyes. "He's a good man."

I nod again, the movement jerky. Henry Stevens is a decent, caring guy. He'll make a good husband, a good father.

"They been together long?" I can't help myself from being a goddamn gossip when I want every morsel of information pertaining to Vivi. Everything and anything I missed over the past seven years, even though I have no right to it, to her, anymore.

Mrs. Cleary tips her head, studying me. "You don't know, do you?"

"Know what?" My voice is hushed, as if the fear of knowing holds it back. Does Vivi hate me? Is she pregnant? Is she in trouble? My throat burns as the thoughts tumble through my mind.

"Henry and Genevieve..." Mrs. Cleary trails off, collecting her thoughts and words, and an irrational surge of dislike rises toward my old friend.

But why shouldn't Henry have Vivi? He stuck around all

these years. He stayed while I…left. Left and never really looked back.

"Well, they're doing right by their families, whatever that means," she says finally, leaving me with more questions. "Come." Mrs. Cleary taps my arm before turning back to the front desk. "Let's get you checked in and showered. Ceremony's at three." She looks up at me. "You have two hours, Declan. Use them."

I nod, following her. Now that I'm here, that strange adrenaline mixed with fear is back, wiping out my fatigue and filling me up with a restlessness that borders on panic.

I need to see Vivi. I need to talk to Henry. I need to mourn Mr. Harrison. I need to know when the hell everything changed so much, and why I didn't realize it until now.

Some of my questions are answered only an hour later as I stand to the side of the church, pacing back and forth, my mind racing. All the emotions of coming home are warring for space in my mind, but I shut them down, focused on Genevieve.

After calling Da to let him know I arrived in Nashville, I quietly enter the church, only to catch my first glimpse of her. And it nearly breaks me.

Genevieve Rae is a vision. She's always been beautiful but now, as a woman, she's stunning. Her golden hair is curled and pulled away from her face, showing off her cheekbones and the delicate slope of her neck. Her lips are a perfect Cupid's bow, begging to be kissed. Her eyes are just as blue as I remember.

But that's where the similarities end. Because the fun-loving, spunky, loud, and giggly girl from my past is now an intense, unreadable force of a woman.

Her voice is even as she stands by the altar, exchanging words with the priest, Father Ward. But she wrings her hands, and I can tell she's nervous, just doing her best to hide it.

Father Ward nods and moves out of the church through a side door. Vivi's shoulders drop a fraction but then the door opens again, and I watch as she straightens, her body tense.

She turns slowly and as she does, she relaxes and a smile that could light up New York City washes over her face. My hands curl into fists as Henry Stevens strides down the aisle. What the hell is he doing here? Isn't it bad luck to see the bride before the wedding?

But nothing about this wedding seems traditional. The timing, the reaction of Mrs. Cleary when she saw me, the bride and the groom meeting before the ceremony, it all indicates a sense of urgency I don't understand.

Henry's expression is serious and Vivi's smile morphs into a look of concern. She holds out her hands as he reaches her. He takes them, pulling her forward to wrap her in a big hug. He holds her for a long moment, both of their eyes closed. They look sad, almost hopeless. Absolutely nothing like a couple about to embark on their happily-ever-after.

Vivi pulls away first but keeps her hands tucked in Henry's. "You can't go through with it, can you?"

"You look beautiful, Viv." Henry kisses both of her cheeks.

I frown, straining to hear their words without giving away my presence. What the hell is going on?

"Henry," Vivi says.

"I can't go through with it," he murmurs, his eyes closing, as if in pain. "I can't live the lie."

"I understand," Vivi states without a trace of anger. "I'm so sorry I ever asked you to."

"No." Henry shakes his head. "I'd do anything for you,

Viv. I just, I *can't* do this. I can't keep hiding like this. I need to tell him."

"It's okay." Vivi shrugs and offers him a lopsided grin.

"It's not," Henry argues with her. He reaches up to stop a tear that falls from her eye and my body coils in anticipation.

Why is she crying? Why is he jilting her? What the hell is he talking about, a lie?

Henry swears and shakes his head. "I hate myself for standing by and watching you lose everything."

"Not everything." She gives him a sad smile.

He shakes his head, his jaw clenched.

"I'll be okay, Henry."

Henry clucks, his expression filled with admiration for Vivi. "Only you, Viv. Only you manage to land on your feet. It's not fair that you're always taking care of everyone, with no one looking out for you. I hate that I'm—"

"Stop," Vivi cuts him off and shakes her head. She clings to his wrist, holding on to him like a lifeline.

I work a swallow, anger rushing through me. Why is she forgiving him so easily for jilting her? Why doesn't she seem angry at all? I'm angry *for* her. And what the hell does Henry mean, no one is looking out for Vivi? Isn't that *his* job, as her fiancé?

"Viv…" Henry cups her cheek, his other hand hooking around her hip to draw her closer. She stumbles forward and I let out a low growl. "You and I both know this is bigger than us. You can't lose the foundation. If Alfred and you…" He trails off and sighs. "So much of the good you're doing will suffer."

Vivi shakes her head, her smile soft, her eyes sad. "But I can't lose you, Henry. I can figure out the foundation stuff and deal with Alfred, but not at the expense of us."

My confusion ratchets up several more notches. Isn't she losing him now? If he leaves her here, in church, on their wedding day, what the hell will be salvageable of their relationship? What am I missing?

Henry clears his throat. "If we do this…"

"Henry, no." Vivi shakes her head. Her eyes close and I watch her shoulders sag. Is she disappointed? Relieved?

Whatever she is, it sure as fuck isn't the fury that races through my body, turning my blood hot. Henry's gonna leave her at the altar? And tell her this on their goddamn wedding day while standing in church?

"Viv…" Henry's thumb swipes along her cheekbone. "You need to get married, babe, and if not me, then who?"

Hurt blazes over Vivi's face, her expression crumpling as Henry's words ring true. It's the dejected acceptance in her eyes that breaks me free of the spell holding my tongue.

I step forward and without thinking about what the hell I'm agreeing to, I announce, "Me."

Read The Trailblazer now!

HEY READER!

Hi there, reader!

Thank you so much for reading *The Heart Chaser*! I hope you loved witnessing player Pandatelli grow into swoony Luca, the family man!

It would mean so much to me if you would please leave a *review* to share your thoughts. If you're loving Boston Hawks Hockey and second chance romances are your thing, *The Trailblazer* is out now!

To be in the know about book news, please subscribe to my monthly newsletter. Or, come hang out in my Facebook Reader Group, Gina's Azzi's Book Besties.

Thank you so much for all your support and for loving the BHH family! It means the world to me!

XO,
    Gina

ACKNOWLEDGMENTS

A million thank you's to the amazing women who have supported this series from day 1! Becca Mysoor, Amy Parsons, Erica Russikoff, and Virginia Carey, *The Heart Chaser* wouldn't exist without your insights, editing expertise, and constant encouragement. Thank you!

All my gratitude to the super talented Kate Farlow, Y'all. That Graphic. for designing covers that I adore!

To MPP for juggling all the things and always being a friend and sounding board. I love working together!

Thank you so much to Dani Sanchez and her awesome team at Wildfire Marketing Solutions and the fabulous women of Give Me Books Promotions for spreading the word about the Boston Hawks!

My sincere thanks to YOU, awesome reader, and all the bloggers, reviewers, and bookstagrammers who adore romance reads. I hope you fell in love with Abbi and Luca.

To my home team, my little heartbeats, love you all the world.

ALSO BY GINA AZZI

Knoxville Coyotes Football:

Faked and Fumbled

Surprised and Sacked

Trapped and Tackled

The Burnt Clovers Trilogy:

Rebellious Rockstar

Resentful Rockstar

Restless Rockstar

Tennessee Thunderbolts:

Hot Shot's Mistake

Brawler's Weakness

Rookie's Regret

Playboy's Reward

Hero's Risk

Bad Boy's Downfall

Lock 'Em Down

Boston Hawks Hockey:

The Sweet Talker

The Risk Taker

The Faker

The Rule Maker

The Defender

The Heart Chaser

The Trailblazer

The Hustler

The Score Keeper

Second Chance Chicago Series:

Broken Lies

Twisted Truths

Saving My Soul

Healing My Heart

The Kane Brothers Series:

Rescuing Broken (Jax's Story)

Recovering Beauty (Carter's Story)

Reclaiming Brave (Denver's Story)

My Christmas Wish

(A Kane Family Christmas

+ *One Last Chance* FREE prequel)

Finding Love in Scotland Series:

My Christmas Wish

(A Kane Family Christmas

+ *One Last Chance* FREE prequel)

One Last Chance (Daisy and Finn)

This Time Around (Aaron and Everly)

One Great Love

The College Pact Series:

The Last First Game (Lila's Story)

Kiss Me Goodnight in Rome (Mia's Story)

All the While (Maura's Story)

Me + You (Emma's Story)

Standalone

Corner of Ocean and Bay